TROLLED

A Shades of Beckwell Novella

SHELLY CHALMERS

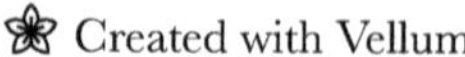
Created with Vellum

For my Family, who are always there to cheer me on… and enjoy cake to celebrate each new book.

And to Grandpa, Uncle Bob, and the gentlemen of the Minnedosa AOTS. This one's for you.

From the Minutes of the S.H.A.D.E.S. (Supernatural Hazard Assessment, Defense & Espionage Section)

"WE ARE the Shades of Beckwell. Though shadows of ourselves, we remain a force to be reckoned with. We take no crap, sugar in our tea, and cookies if you have them.

Alteration of our charter:

Requisite for becoming a SHADES member:

~~**1.** *over the age of fifty*~~

2. *possession of magical or paranormal ability and/or heritage*

3. *a sincere desire to protect and defend Beckwell and our families regardless of the amount of interference or prodding this may require.*

Mission 1: It has become apparent the gods are still being twits and our town faces new threats. It is time to begin recruitment…"

Chapter One

Frizzly

My cat was out to kill me. Either that, or turn me into a man-size lawn-ornament, neither of which was on my to-do list. Freaking cat. Standing on my front stoop, I shielded my eyes with a hand and squinted up at the sun rising higher and higher in the sky, blasting my entire yard with sunlight. I hid in the shade and clenched the towel more tightly around my waist, since the second the sun touched me, I'd be turned to stone, which was a really crappy way to start a Tuesday. The smart thing to do would be go inside, get dressed, cover every inch of skin, *then* venture out after Mr. Whiskers.

A dark silhouette, wings stretched wide, circled above with deadly intent, or at least hungry intent. *Damn it, damn it, damn it.* This was why Mr. Whiskers was supposed to stay inside, so he didn't end up eagle chow.

"Ah, hell." I clucked my tongue desperately and scanned the yard, the waning green that came with late summer. "Here, Mr. Whiskers! Come on, you little bugger. Come inside and I'll give you some of that fish from last night. Hell, I'll give you the whole damned fish. Here, Mr. Whiskers. Come on, kitty."

Where the hell was he? And how had he gotten out this time? I scanned the open driveway and yard, not a sign of the orange tabby. He wasn't over by my rosebushes, the last of the flowers blooming their heart out and raining delicate pink petals onto the lawn. Not even digging up my petunias. The surrounding trees and woodland were dense —full of things that would love to eat my cat.

Then there were the other neighborhood cats. He had a better love life than I did, and I was pretty sure the neighbors didn't appreciate that fact. Which was why I'd been careful to close all the windows last night, checked them again this morning. All closed. Unless Mr. Whiskers had developed opposable thumbs or the ability to open window latches overnight, he should have been safe inside.

Then again, this was Beckwell, home of the paranormal, magic, and the four horsewomen of the apocalypse. Stranger things had happened.

The silhouette above grew larger as the eagle circled lower. Even if I couldn't see the damned cat, I bet the bird could.

"Mr. Whiskers! Come on, kitty. Come on inside. Here, kitty, kitty, kitty!" I called again, desperately. Still no sign of the bugger. The muscles in my shoulders bunched. How long did I have? Long enough to throw something over all my exposed skin first?

"Kitty, where are you going?" a female voice said from somewhere to the left of the house.

I didn't have time to wonder about her.

There was a small meow, and my orange fluff ball bounded out of the nearby bushes.

The eagle dove.

I raced out into the sun.

The rays touched my flesh with icy chills that spread down through my pores, stabbed deep into muscle tissue.

I stumbled, my steps slowing, my gaze glued to the little orange fuzzball.

Hell, would I even reach Mr. Whiskers in time? Or end up only able to watch, turned to stone as the eagle swooped in and carried him off for lunch.

I was still two steps away when the eagle screamed, talons launched, ready to scoop up Mr. Whiskers.

Only to dissolve, mid-screech, into rainbow-hued bubbles that glinted in the sun.

A small, dark-skinned, dark-haired woman scooped up Mr. Whiskers and almost collided with me as she raced for the house. She craned her neck up to see my face and scowled, the look oddly incongruous with her delicate features. She grabbed my arm with her free hand and dragged me in her wake.

I stumbled after her, the vision in my right eye a bit wonky, blurring the way it did when I forgot my sunglasses and part of my retina turned to stone.

The door slammed behind us, and Mr. Whiskers chirruped as the strange woman let him down onto the floor.

She kept dragging me onward, still her captive even in my own house. She muttered to herself as we went, but on the part of my arm that hadn't turned to granite, her small fingers trembled against my tattooed skin. I caught something about bird and town and mission, but pretty sure one of my ears had turned to stone, judging from the cold numbness of it, so what did I know?

We ended up in my living room, where Mr. Whiskers scampered up to the top of his four-foot cat tree, then along the carpet-covered running rails along the wall, mostly, I was pretty sure, just so he could meow directly in my face.

"You're supposed to stay inside, little buddy," I said, my voice gravelly. I lowered myself into the me-sized reclining chair with its worn blue upholstery, grimacing at every unbending joint. My back and shoulders seemed to have taken the brunt of the sunlight, since my muscles were immobile, and the deep chill of stone compressed my chest and made it hard to breathe.

Crap. I was due at work in two hours at the Beckwell med clinic working the front desk, something I both enjoyed and was damned good at. I frowned at my right hand that lay on the armrest. My rose-thorn tattoos looked like stone etchings along the length of my upper arm, the flesh of my biceps resembling a granite statue more than it looked human. But my hand had taken the worst of the sunlight, so much so that the granite statue-look of my upper arm transitioned into a craggy lump that barely resembled a hand. It'd be useless for filing reports today, answering the phone, or dealing with patients.

I frowned at the woman staring at me. Yes, she'd just rescued Mr. Whiskers, and quite possibly me. But I knew practically everyone in town.

I didn't know her.

"Thanks for the rescue. Who are you exactly?" I said, voice still gravelly.

She was gorgeous, a brown-skinned goddess with dark brown, slightly tilted eyes who'd somehow blasted into my life with greater radiance then the sun. She cocked her head, dark hair pulled up in one of those half-ponytail, half-bun things women did. Her hair slid sideways, brushing the shoulder of her sapphire and gold scarf draped over a similarly colored blouse. "I'm Devi. So what are you? Vampire? Gargoyle?" She sounded fascinated, like she'd just encountered an especially intriguing specimen.

She also hadn't answered my question. Not really. Beckwell was generally a pretty welcoming place, but we also got the occasional kooks who wanted to destroy us. Plus, I was half turned to stone and wearing only a towel. Crud. I couldn't even rescue my cat, let alone myself. But, as Dad had always reminded me, I was more than just my muscles. I wanted to prove I could be a man he could be proud of. I'd play her game and see what I could find out, then pass it on to someone who could deal with her if she was here to cause trouble.

"Don't vampires get sunburns? I'm a troll. Well, half troll." I was babbling a little. Never said this much usually. But I'd never sneakily interrogated anyone, let alone a beautiful woman in my house. "What happened to the eagle back there? They don't usually disappear into bubbles." Which meant she had power. Power wasn't good. Especially not in strangers.

Geezus, living in Beckwell during these tumultuous times was starting to turn me into the suspicious guy I'd been back in the biker gang.

She sat back in the chair, pink darkening her cheekbones. "Oh, that, well, you know. I transmuted him. The plan was to turn him into dust, but…" She looked down at her lap, where she fiddled with the edge of the decorative gold and sapphire scarf that draped over her shoulders, then looked up with a forced smile. "Aren't trolls supposed to be all big, ugly, and stup—" She snapped her lips closed, deep color staining her cheekbones. "Gee, you have a really nice, uh, what is this room again? No bed… Is this a parlour? A room used for reception and conversation with guests, correct?"

"It sounds like you read that from a book. One about the mortal world I'm guessing?"

She gave a small nod.

Which meant I was right—she wasn't from around here. And if she was new to the mortal or human world, that made her likely to be either from what had formerly been Braelyn, world of the gods, fairies, and the like. Or Daimoleigh, home of the demons. Not that either of them existed anymore, what with the Veils coming down a few months back because of the four horsewomen. But that also made her more likely to be dangerous. Especially if she was a god or related to them.

They had this thing with trying to wipe Beckwell off the face of the planet.

I took a deep breath but figured I had to address the troll comment. "I take it what you've heard about trolls hasn't been especially positive." It's not like I hadn't heard every troll joke and slur before, but on behalf of myself and Mom's people, the fight to end prejudice had to start somewhere. "Most trolls aren't big on social interaction, so most people have never met a troll. We're almost anti-magical; spells and such don't tend to work on us—maybe because of the rock part—and some of us have limited precognition abilities. Then there's the turning to stone in the sun part. But our intelligence isn't based on our species, no more than anyone else."

She bit her lip and stole a glance up at me through her lashes. I'd have figured it for a ploy to get me to forgive her the slight if she didn't seem so otherwise guileless—I don't think she was even wearing makeup. Then again, acting innocent was a really good way to get away with things.

"I-I'm sorry," she practically whispered. "I've never met a real troll. I don't think I've even read about one before." She jumped up, rubbing her hands down her colorful dress. "I have wronged you and must make amends. Do you have a…" Another lip nibble.

Damn. She had nice lips. Like the kind movie-stars could only wish for…and the kind that gave a guy ideas. Bad ideas.

Hello. Stranger? Likely here to cause trouble, if she followed the pattern most of our past new arrivals had.

She was frowning now, seemingly searching for the right term. "It's where food preparation and storage happen. I believe it starts with a 'g.'"

"Uh, pretty sure you mean the kitchen. Look, you don't have to do anything—although I'd really like to know who you are, what brings you to—"

"Kitchen! Yes, that's it," she interrupted me, before her joy quickly gave way to a scowl. "That doesn't start with a 'g' at all, does it?" Her expression cleared, and she gestured over her shoulder, already moving back out into the hall that led off from the front door and the living room. My house wasn't huge.

"It's back there. But wait—"

She'd already headed out of the arched doorway of my living room. "I'll just help myself to a little frankincense, Vertruvian peppercorn, and nightcrawler. Whatever you have on hand," she called back.

Definitely not from around here. "I don't have any of those things," I called back. I glanced down at my body. I was naked, wearing only a towel, and still mostly stone. Shit. "Why don't we just talk?" I tried again. "I could tell you lots of interesting things about town. I'd love to hear what brings you here."

"Aha! I have found the food— I mean, the kitchen," she called back. A moment or two later, she returned from down the hall, popping her head around the arched entrance to the living room. "What about Jabberknoll feathers? Fluxweed?"

"Nope, sorry. Look, I—"

"Oh! Silly me. This is the mortal realm." With a flash of a smile, she disappeared back around the corner again, likely headed for my kitchen, her voice trailing back. "It's so strange, getting used to it all, without the Veils. So, what about camel dung-dust? Maybe some Swedish pansy-leaf?"

That sealed it. I had a visitor formally of Braelyn or Daimoleigh—either the realm of the gods or the realm of the demons, all of which had been squashed back into one world with the "mortal realm" when the four horsewomen had switched things up. Long story short, the crap spread around about demons was about as accurate as the shit people said about trolls. Not all of them had horns, they were no more evil than the average person, and for the most part, they'd rather be left alone than try to take over the world. I wasn't especially concerned if I met a stray demon, since those poor suckers were just looking for safe sanctuary.

Unfortunately, I didn't take the woman for a demon.

Which left the former-god world, filled with angels, gods, and half-gods, most of them conceited. Now, if you were looking for someone with an ego complex who was likely to take over the world, try one of them. Not big fans of Beckwell or any of us that lived here, either. Mostly, they wanted us all erased from existence.

So…why'd she save Mr. Whiskers? Or help me back into the house?

It could be part of her ploy somehow. Plus, all this sexy-innocent stuff. My stomach twisted—the part that still could and wasn't turned to stone—because I didn't want her to be into anything bad. But she'd also so far ignored most of my questions.

"Tawnymoth weed. You must have some of that?" she called out again.

I lifted my sole-functioning hand—gravity kept the towel in place—and rubbed my eyes. How would one of the Four or even Loki handle a situation like this? I was an office administrator, for frick's sake. I wasn't the one you came to with big problems. Troll and all, I'd too often become the bad stereotype, a magnet for violence. These days, I kept my head down, didn't get involved, focused on being kind. Someone I could face in the mirror.

"Nope, no tawnymoth weed—and I'll head you off by saying whatever you'll ask for next? I probably don't have it, either. That's my kitchen. Where I cook mostly edible things, or at least microwave them. No special herbs more exotic than oregano, and the fridge is probably empty, too. I was supposed to stop for groceries after work today. But help yourself to whatever you find." I scowled down at my body, at least a third of me turned to rock. I straightened, dropping my hand, an idea striking me. "Afraid I'm not going anywhere soon. But if you do want to help, would you mind grabbing me my phone? I was supposed to be at work, but I'd better call the boss man, tell him I won't be in."

While I was at it, I'd clue in my boss, the town doctor, on what was going on. He was married to one of the four horsewomen—pestilence, ironically. Since the merging of the worlds, the Four had mostly been in charge, or were trying to be, along with the town founder, Loki. The gods had been trying to cause mayhem and destruction for the past few months, but even without them, things were a mess. Magic was back in the mortal world and out in the open. We had arrivals from out of town who'd just found out they had paranormal abilities. There was the occasional news crew, even human tourists. This woman seemed nice enough, but lots of those who'd shown up to cause trouble before had seemed nice enough…until Beckwell residents ended up caught in the crossfire.

Besides which, if she refused to get me my phone, that'd say something about her intentions, wouldn't it?

Surprisingly, she popped back around the corner. "Phone?" She looked around. "Communication device. Often portable, very sensitive to magic…" She murmured to herself, as though rattling off a definition she'd read somewhere, but she spotted my phone on the ledge near the door, grabbed it, and brought it over to me with a smile.

"You do that a lot, don't you? Depend on what you've read to understand this place. Have you ever been to the mortal realm before?" I reached for the phone with my good hand.

Our fingertips brushed, and small sparks of sensation zapped through me like fireworks during Beckwell Days. I forgot how to breathe, was probably just staring at her. Trolls were—other than our sensitivity to the sun—immune to most magic. So whatever happened between us when we touched… Hell if I knew what that'd been.

She sucked in a breath, freezing and studying me from beneath those long lashes. Her gaze slid up from my legs, over the towel, up my stomach, along my chest, shoulders, until her dark eyes finally met mine. A small breath escaped from between her lips. "This is my first time for a lot of new things today," she murmured.

Did she have any idea of the sexual connotations I read into that comment?

She looked at me like there was something interesting to see. Something other than the crooked nose broken in too many fights and red hair that called even more attention to me. Like someone over six and a half feet needed any more attention. I quickly adjusted my towel in the least-creepy-possible way, seeing as it was covering my crotch.

"Well," she said, voice breathy, studying me like something between an exciting new specimen and maybe a large chocolate sundae with a cherry on top she was about to devour. "They definitely did have the big part right when it comes to trolls, hmm?"

I could only stare. Oh gods. She might be here to cause harm to my town, but she'd already destroyed my sanity. And better sense. I was having trouble thinking with my big head. "I, uh…"

Fortunately, she spun away before I could humiliate myself further.

"That stone looks uncomfortable and painful on the joints." She turned on her heel and headed from the room. "I'll check the nourishment center and see what I can do to help before I get back to work. I can't mess up my first official mission."

Chapter Two

CALL ME PARANOID, BUT THE "MISSION" Devi mentioned sure made it sound like she was in Beckwell for other purposes. Nefarious ones, if history were any indication.

Alone once more, I let out a long, unsteady breath, lowered my phone in my lap and loosened my grip on the towel. I dropped my head against the chair, massaging my forehead. This was not how I'd expected the day to go. These days, my life was predictable, and I liked it that way. Work, my bike Edith, Mr. Whiskers, garden, sleep, repeat. You kept your head down and the whispers and looks mostly stopped. Even in a town as paranormal and large as Beckwell, I was the former biker and only troll. Most of Mom's people were the definition of wild mountain man, preferring solitary life to society, and I got that…but something always kept me here, always at the edge of the crowd, trying to prove to everyone I wasn't like the troll stereotypes. I could be kind, gentle, never hurt a soul. Which was easy so long as I was never part of the action.

Until today. When a gorgeous woman crashed into my

yard and life, who'd saved Mr. Whiskers and me but talked about missions. You know who else talked about those? People who came here and tried to murder the Four or other people I cared about. Sure, I didn't know for certain that Devi's "mission" was dangerous. But I couldn't risk people getting hurt, and if she was here to cause trouble, that was way above my pay grade. Protecting Beckwell, being the hero, that required action and getting involved, probably fists and violence, things that'd turn me into the stereotype I didn't like.

Nope and nope.

From the kitchen at the back of the house, cupboards opened and closed with soft thuds. If I strained, I caught Devi's soft murmurs, the sucking sound of the fridge door opening.

Mr. Whiskers jumped down from his perch above my head and raced after the woman. Or more accurately, the possibility of food.

Maybe this was a nightmare. Or some new kind of torture. I sucked when it came to dating and romance, but the way she looked at me? Pretty sure my guest was attracted to me, at least a little. I would not be the creep who got hard in front of her…at least, you know, not harder in the parts that mattered. Yeah, I'd heard all those jokes about trolls and hardness, too. But maybe she hadn't. She looked at me like I was more than just a stereotype. She looked at me like I was a man.

I glanced at my phone. Was her pseudo attraction part of the trick? I sighed, and with the phone in my lap, started to dial the Med Center, one of several services located in the Beckwell Senior Center. After pushing send, I picked up the phone and held it to my remaining good ear to wait for an answer.

I didn't want to get Devi in trouble, but Beckwell was

home. This had to be a place where people were safe, no matter what they looked like, who, or what they were. The clinic wouldn't open for another hour or so, but the doc did rounds for the residents every morning before shift. So why was the phone just ringing unanswered?

"Um, your cat is in the cold box food holder," the woman called from the next room while I listened to the call ring through. "Should he be in there?"

I took this to mean Mr. Whiskers had climbed into the fridge again. Probably after the fish. If he wasn't out to turn me into stone, he usually seemed bent on his own destruction. I hadn't yet decided if it was because he was exceptionally intelligent or really, really dumb. "No, he shouldn't be. You can give him some of the fish, though, if you wouldn't mind. I promised him. Just make sure there aren't any bones. He eats so fast he could choke."

"Oh. Okay." She called the cat. Then argued with the cat. There were a few more mutters before porcelain hit the tile floor and the fridge finally closed.

"Mornin', Frizzly," came the cheerful voice on the other end of the line, instantly making me narrow my eyes and focus on the phone call.

It wasn't the doc or one of the regulars at the nursing station.

It was one of the residents.

My seniors-up-to-trouble antenna made the back of my neck itch. "Morning, Mr. Jenklow," I said slowly. "Why are you answering the Center phone line? Is Doc Quilan around?"

From the kitchen, there was the sound of cupboards opening and closing, then hushed cursing. I didn't have time to fool around this morning. I needed help with the Devi situation.

Albert Jenklow was one of the Senior Center residents,

and I liked him and most of the others. I did. But fact was, they were there because no one else could handle them. They might have been old, some of them infirm, but age did little to diminish their powers. If you took away their wands and staffs, they just made new ones out of their walkers, canes, and false teeth. Jenklow in particular was a good guy, sweet smile, something nice to say to everyone… and one of the biggest troublemakers. He and his friends, all retired former military buddies, called themselves the "Shades." They were like a biker gang that had gotten old…and much more dangerous.

"Oh, Jenny's son has the sniffles today, the poor mite, so I said I'd cover until Maria could get here," Jenklow said, cheerful as always and spiking my suspicion that the nursing staff had been conveniently indisposed. Hell. I did not need to deal with the Shades launching a coup at the Center.

A chill stole through me, similar to the chill of forming stone, but worse. In Beckwell, it was considered rude to ask people right out what their abilities and heritage were. Kind of specist. But I'd seen most of the patient files. I knew Mr. Jenklow was related to Baba Yaga, old sorcery, and had a long record of trouble-making that had more than once gotten him various injuries and an extensive medical record. Likely a criminal one, too. He "knew" things sometimes, limited precognition. I'd seen stuff in the office that suggested long before my or Doc Quilan's time, Jenklow had even helped on the medical side of things, a healer of some variety. Pretty sure Jenklow meant "trouble" in another language.

I tapped the phone for a second against my forehead before finding the strength to keep my tone even. I'd dealt with the seniors enough to know whatever you did, never show weakness. They could smell fear, just like velociraptors and small children. I kept my tone conversational. "Gee, that's great you were there to fill in. Can you get the doc on the phone, now please? How about your granddaughter, Cara?"

Cara Jenklow also worked at the Center, and we'd gone to school together. Sometimes she could handle the Shades, maybe because she was related.

Mr. Jenklow hummed a little. "Cara has the day off. Are you having a difficult morning, Frizzly?"

My eyes narrowed, and I gripped the phone. "My cat got out this morning. Any idea how that happened? And—"

A crash came from the kitchen, followed by cursing in a language I didn't recognize. The small boom of an explosion cut off my words.

Mr. Whiskers raced into the living room, tail puffed up.

I lowered the phone to call out. "Everything okay in there?" Geezus. She wouldn't start an attack on Beckwell from my kitchen, would she?

"Oh, yes. Fine, fine." Devi popped her head into the room, her pretty face covered in white powder that frosted her eyelashes, an over-wide smile straining her lips. "Did you know baking soda and knotgrass explode when combined? I didn't." She disappeared back around the corner before I could respond.

"Frizzly? Dear boy, are you still there?" Mr. Jenklow was speaking loud enough I could hear him even without holding up the phone. "Have you ever considered getting a dog? They come when they're called. Or perhaps a fish. I imagine you're using up that 400SPF sunblock my Cara brewed up far too quickly otherwise."

Reluctantly, I moved the phone back to my ear, still frowning at the now empty doorway. I better get in that kitchen soon. While I still had one. "Sorry. Here. Did you know that knotgrass and baking soda explode when combined?" I said, somewhat bemusedly.

"Of course. Simple chemistry, son. Same thing with sugar and bellamy. Always a bit unstable if it's potent enough."

I lowered the phone again. "Watch out for sugar and bellamy, too," I called.

"Oh! Really?" Again she popped her head around the corner. Her face was no longer covered in white powder, and she held what appeared to be a mortar and pestle in one hand. She gave me a quick grin. "I'll have to remember that."

She returned to the kitchen, and I lifted the phone. Between the possible goddess who might blow Mr. Whiskers, me, and my house sky high and Jenklow, my B.S. tolerance was tapped out for the day. "Time for straight-talk and truth, Mr. Jenklow. Did you let my cat out this morning? What did you do with the doc? I need to talk to him because I have a new guest who I'm pretty sure is from what was formerly Braelyn, and who turned an eagle into bubbles."

"Doctor Quilan is just fine—home with his teething twins who are beginning to manifest their first abilities. Listen carefully. Your guest is potentially dangerous. Heimdall warned us a powerful demi-goddess might end up in town and would likely target the Senior Center and central Beckwell. She's gifted in transmogrification, portals, and reality bubbles, and is likely on a mission of destruction. Has she tried to harm you?" Mr. Jenklow's voice had grown serious in a way that would have raised the hairs on the back of my neck if they hadn't been as stone as my skin.

"Other than trying to blow up my house? No. Heimdall told *you* all this?"

"Well…technically he told Loki, which was overheard by Loki's manservant Trevor, who told us when we bribed him with our histories. He's a sucker for a good biography. Never mind that. Find out what you can. Try not to get turned into bubbles…or anything else."

"Now listen here, Mr. Jenklow," I interrupted, using my best "the doctor will see you when he is available and only then" voice. "I'm not part of these games, you hear me? I like boring, I like normal, I like not being involved. Which also means leave Mr. Whiskers out of it. You can bribe Loki's servants, not me. Find someone else. Tell the Doc. Or one of the Four. Or—"

Jenklow continued like he hadn't heard me, or more likely, didn't care. "When you're able to, bring her here to us. We'll help. Good job, Frizzly. I knew I was right about you." The line went dead.

I pulled it away from my ear and glared down at it before the "call ended" notification disappeared, showing only my apps and the screensaver of Mr. Whiskers. What the hell had Jenklow and his cronies gotten me into?

"All right, let's try this," Devi said, coming back into the room with a smile. She'd lost her long decorative scarf somewhere along the way, now wearing only a tight-fitting blouse-thing that clung to her curves—and she had curves in all the right places—along with some kind of wide, silky-looking pants that also seemed to cling and then flutter away, hinting at the curves of her legs.

She knelt in front of me between my knees with a small bowl full of green goop.

My brain stuttered and shut off. I dropped my phone, and it hit the carpet with a dull thud, which I could barely hear above the racing of my heart and the rush of my blood through my veins. Towel. *Towel.* I was still freaking naked. Was it, uh, positioned correctly so that I didn't look like the creep I felt like? Because even parts that hadn't been exposed to the sun were definitely getting a, ahem, granite feeling.

It didn't help when she started to smooth the green goop on a patch of gray-spotted granite on my thigh. An escaped curl of hair brushed my skin as she leaned over to study her work.

I sucked in a breath. I should have stopped her. Jenklow had as much confirmed she was probably dangerous. Definitely should have said something about appropriate physical distancing for strangers and the like. But my tongue wasn't working, swallowing was difficult, and I tried to delicately adjust the lay of my towel, kind of bunch it up a bit.

"Yes! It's working." She looked up at me with a wide grin, a sparkle in those dark eyes. A soft flush stained her cheekbones, and she pushed back that escaped lock of hair, tucking it behind her ear. She'd smeared some of the green goop on her cheek.

Gods, she was beautiful. And adorable, even if she had possibly blown up my kitchen. Her touch was just as soft as I'd imagined, and damn, but it'd been a long time since I'd been touched. Wonder what would happen if I asked her out for a date? Like, a real one, with dinner and maybe…uh…

Earth to Frizzly. Enemy? Danger to Beckwell? This was a setup. I had to—

"You're getting all tense. Does it hurt? I was sure it was working," she said, softly prodding my thigh.

Her fingertip seemed to sink gently into malleable flesh and muscle.

Hang on—I *felt* that. My gaze fell to my thigh, where beneath the smear of green goop my thigh was definitely looking more flesh and bone rather than granite and stone.

"How'd you do that?" I breathed out, testing the skin with a finger. It was completely back to normal. "It usually takes almost a week to reverse the stone, even with Cara's special lotion."

"Oh, well, my brothers and sisters and I used to accidentally—and sometimes on purpose—turn each other stone all the time when we were kids. Dad's part basilisk. Learning how to turn someone into stone is easy. Learning to control those powers takes more practice. My brothers and sisters were never interested in things that required practice." She shrugged and continued smoothing. "I got pretty good at making the salve to turn them back."

I grabbed her hand a moment because I couldn't think straight with her touching me. Those fireworks went off again and I struggled to focus. "Look, this is really kind of you. But I need you to answer some questions for me. Like, other than 'Devi,' what's your name and why are you here in Beckwell? Hell, why are you even here in my house? I mean, still in my house? I appreciate you helping Mr. Whiskers and me, but I have to say, I'm confused as hell and more than a little concerned." And turned-on, but I left that part out.

Her shoulders sagged a bit and she regarded me seriously. "I told you, I'm Devi. Dad's family was part basilisk, that's how I know about the stone stuff. And you hardly introduced yourself." She stood, pulling away. "Your back seems to be the worst, but I can't reach it with you sitting like that. I think I saw a chair in the kitchen." Leaving her bowl of goop behind, she padded off toward the kitchen.

I braced myself for what she was going to grab and looked around. She could grab a knife. That'd hurt if she found anything that wasn't stone. What did I have to defend myself with? My bare hands, sure. I'd been in enough fights back in the biker gang. It'd been a combo of

Norms—non-magicals—and gnomes, so I was the biggest guy, aka the muscle, and even if gnomes could drink anyone under a table thanks to their two livers, they usually caused plenty of trouble before they passed out. But fists got me involved in ways I wasn't comfortable with. Never mind that bad guy or not, I couldn't hit a lady, especially not Devi. Yes, of course, I knew who was really the stronger sex—it wasn't men—but still.

I looked around, but other than the TV remote, there was nothing within reach. What if she let more enemies in through the back door? I didn't know for sure that she'd come here alone. *Dammit, dammit, dammit.* Why did Jenklow and his cronies have to play their games today? I could really have used some backup myself. Like people who were used to dealing with this kind of stuff. Give me intake papers, filing, and a cranky waiting room any day. This was nuts.

"Here, this should work," she said just before she entered the room.

She held one of my kitchen chairs, which she placed near the middle of the room, then patted it.

"Do you need some help getting up?"

No, I needed help with this whole damned situation. "I can do it."

I clutched my towel and slowly managed to lever myself into first a standing position, then shuffled the few steps to the kitchen chair. In the center of the room, without the bulk of the easy chair as protection, I was excruciatingly exposed, but getting dressed while still stone would hurt more. I lowered myself into the chair, unable to stifle the groan when other muscles had to make up for my increased weight and the fact that too many other muscles weren't doing anything other than being hard, rocky lumps. My chest and back pressed against my lungs, preventing me from taking a deep breath. My knees didn't bend properly, so I collapsed down in the chair that groaned but held under my weight.

I sighed, partially with impatience, partially with relief that I wasn't standing anymore. "Look. I can't do this all day. Can I get some answers? Please? I'm Frizzly Cooper. This is my house. You met my cat. Now it's your turn."

"Grizzly? Like the North American bear species?" Her face lit up and her gaze met mine, as though very pleased she'd connected something she'd read about and reality.

It sucked to have to dim that glow. "Uh, no, not Grizzly. Frizzly. Dad wanted a traditional troll name to connect me to my heritage and stuff, but he'd never actually met a troll other than my mom, and this leprechaun totally lied to him." Ah, hell. I was oversharing because she still knelt in front of me, her free hand absently on my knee, rubbing in that goop. I cleared my throat, voice gruff. "It's Frizzly. Like Grizzly, but with an 'F.'"

Gods, what they said about trolls might not be true in general, but it definitely was true about me today. Dense and stupid as a rock.

"Are leprechauns sneaky like they say then? And didn't your mother explain the truth to your father?"

"Mom left me at the hospital after I was born with a note for Dad. Never saw her again. And no, lots of leprechauns are probably very nice and honest. But not Ronald O'Reilly. He was our neighbor and a lying jerk. You haven't answered any of my questions. Don't you have a last name? What about why you're here? Let's start there."

She tugged her hand free of mine, then scooped up some more green goop and reached for my chest. "I don't have a last name. Just Devi. Devi the Destroyer officially. At least, kind of. I mean, that's kind of my…let's call her my grandmother for simplicity's sake, right? Or Bibiji. She's the real Devi. I was just named after her." Her fingers moved in deep, massaging circles down my shoulders.

"Grandmother, huh?" My voice was rough, but nothing I could do about that. I wiggled fingers that now once more resembled fingers. "Sounds like a heck of a name to live up to." It sounded like the kind of name a goddess would have. A dangerous one. This was definitely bad. But how the heck would I get her to the Senior Center without raising her suspicions?

"I've never met her, actually. She was always so busy. And my parents didn't see the point in introducing me." There was a frown in her voice, and when she started smoothing the salve into my left shoulder, her touch was a little less gentle. "Why I got her name, I don't know. Perhaps my parents should have waited a while, until my abilities manifested. I mean, my sister Narissa? She'd have been a much better Devi. She once burned my bedroom to ash when she used to use her abilities. Or Parvi? He's my little brother. He once turned our entire garden into a barren desert. But he doesn't really do that anymore. Lean forward, will you? So I can reach lower on your back."

I tried to comply, stiffly, while simultaneously trying to make sense of her words. I'd never had siblings myself, but I'd seen that kind of tension between them lots of time. Even between the doc and his twin brother, before they'd both gotten married and made peace with each other.

"So you're part basilisk, part destruction goddess," I said gruffly, hyper aware of her as she moved closer and began smoothing the salve into my right shoulder.

Warmth returned with tingles at first, then the feel of her fingertips on my flesh…which caused its own problems, but whatever. She was behind me at least, leaving the towel a little less responsible for all decency and non-creepiness.

"That's some resume," I continued, as she didn't add anything. "What brings you to Beckwell then?" My neck was mostly flesh again, and I turned to look at her. "You don't have to smooth in the lotion yourself, you know. I can do it." Maybe I could think clearer if she wasn't touching me.

She raised a brow but held out the bowl of goop. "It'll be faster if I help. Unless you want to stay stone for the rest of the day, unable to move and miserable."

The look she gave me made me feel like I was clearly the dumbest troll in existence, refusing to allow a beautiful woman to rub her hands all over my body. Even if it did feel like somehow I was taking advantage of her innocence. Maybe she didn't know how things worked in the mortal world.

Mr. Whiskers chimed in from above with a meow, calling me "dummy" in cat.

I grumbled to myself about beautiful strangers and death-wish cats. "I'll do the front, you do the back." I scooped out some of the goop, sniffing at it a bit before rubbing it into my bad arm, starting with the biceps and working my way down to the hand. It didn't feel nearly as good as when she did it, but stone slowly gave way to skin.

Meanwhile, she continued to work on my back. "I'm here because of a new job, actually. First assignment, first official mission. At least, I think it's a job? See, there was some craziness with my last employer, so I took the buyout package. Which meant yet again, I got 'the look' from Mother and Father. My sister recommended this other employer, and they said if I proved myself with this first mission here in Beckwell, I'd be going places."

Yep, that was definitely working. I could feel more and

more of her touch…and it was becoming harder and harder not to react to it.

Shit. What had she said? New job. More about the mission. What the heck kind of jobs did goddesses take? "Aren't goddesses just worshipped?" I stifled a groan at how good her hands felt on my back. Reminding myself she was potentially a homicidal maniac wasn't helping. Clearly, my death-wish cat and I had more in common than I thought.

"Only real goddesses. I'm a descendant. My family and I… Well, more my family than me, we live off of Bibiji's faith-energy. The more worshippers a god has, the more power or access to magic they have, so the more they can do. We get it in kind of a trickle-down effect. Devi the Destroyer is still widely worshipped." Her shoulders slumped, and her brow furrowed. "The real Devi, I mean. My family usually just calls me Devi the Useless. That's why I have to prove myself with this new job. I have to get it right. Show them I'm worthy."

What the hell kind of parent called their child useless? Protectiveness clawed at me, and I scowled. Maybe it was all part of her cover, a way to garner sympathy. She was finally talking, and I had to get her to tell me more about this new job—and who exactly she was working for. Did she mean USELESS? USELESS was the gods' version of the KGB or Hitler's SS. Except less friendly and one hundred percent out to destroy Beckwell and everyone in it. Crap. Their agents came here on "missions." My stomach—the parts that weren't stone—tightened, which made the parts that were stone pull, which made everything hurt.

"So who are these new employers of yours anyway? Are they treating you right? And what kind of mission could bring you all the way out to Beckwell? I love Beckwell, trust me, but if it was my first time in the mortal realm, there are a few places that might be higher on my list." There were higher-value targets than a small town like Beckwell.

Even if we did have the four horsewomen of the apocalypse. And Loki. Countless other paranormal families. Plenty of new paranormal refugees. And a growing following online. Crud.

Plus, USELESS might take their defeat at the hands of the Four personally and have come to even the score. Double crud.

Both her hands slid down my back, almost as low as my hips.

I couldn't help it. All thought other than her touch faded to the background. I groaned at how damned good it felt.

She froze. "Are you okay? Am I hurting you?"

Crap, crap, crap. I'd been just about to get some real answers before my lust got in the way. "Uh, yeah. Sure. Are you?"

Mr. Whiskers meowed up above us, totally laughing at me, the ungrateful furball.

"Should I…? Oh dear. This was a mistake, wasn't it? Oh, great job, Devi. Show everyone how clueless you are. Gods, they'll all love to hear about this back home. How clueless Devi blundered into yet another mistake." She came around front of me. Her face had darkened with crimson, and she barely peeked up at me through her lashes, her hands picking at her shirt, spreading green goop everywhere. "Mortals don't…massage each other frequently, do they?"

"Uh…" I said, clearly proving my intelligence as I tried to decide how to explain…and maybe still somehow not make her stop touching me. Plus, answers. Was this innocence a ploy, or was it just part of her? Either way, it was screwing with my brain in ways I'd never experienced. It'd been a long, long time since any woman had given me more than a passing glance and I'd ended up anywhere fun. I'd never been anyone's first choice. Which was probably why, instead of demanding answers like I should have done, I tried to explain and relieve her embarrassment.

"Usually, before massage, there's, uh, a few more introductions first?" My face heated.

"Ah. This is why you've been asking so many questions?"

She said it so guilelessly, that deep-brown gaze so open, I knew if there was a hell, I was definitely going to it if I took advantage of her.

Frick's sake. She'd openly told me most of why she was here. She'd been nothing but kind so far. Jenklow had said I was supposed to find out about her, but I'd only found out her name and that she probably worked for someone out to cause trouble. Concerns? Yeah, I had plenty of those, but probably not the kind I was supposed to have, since more of them had to do with the diminutive size of my towel and the effects of her sweet touch.

Dad always said if in doubt, kindness and honesty were always the right policy. Which had often made me wonder exactly how he'd ever ended up in bed with a troll…or maybe that was exactly why. There'd been times in my life when I hadn't followed that policy, like when I'd been part of that biker gang and I'd let everyone believe I was exactly what everyone accused me of—big, strong, and stupid—and I'd lived my life accordingly. Violence found me, I got involved, people got hurt. Served me right that pretty much everything had gone to shit. Dad's policy guided my life these days, as it had to.

"Generally, people don't give each other massages

unless they're professionals at it." I thought of explaining the difference between the different kinds of "professionals" who might give massages but quickly decided against it. "Or…they're in a relationship. Probably an intimate one."

Her face scrunched up. "Intimate…" It was almost like I could see her checking it against whatever the hell she'd read and learned about the mortal world because I was getting the idea she hadn't spent much time in it. "Meaning if I answer all of your questions, we'll then know each other very well and that will constitute a relationship?"

I cleared my throat awkwardly and shifted in the chair. "Er, maybe. I definitely want answers to those questions." I needed to get her to Jenklow and people who actually dealt with this kind of stuff and didn't get distracted by seemingly sweet destruction goddesses and their soft hands. "And…I mean, uh, the people generally know each other physically." Ah, hell. I blew out a breath. "I mean sex, Devi. Physical intercourse. Don't they have that where you come from?" I'd heard stories about gods' children springing from their heads and stuff, but that couldn't be true, could it?

Her brows lifted and realization slid over her face. Then a flash of hot color. "Oh. I mean…of course, we do. I just… We don't…or at least I don't…" She cleared her throat and lifted her shoulders. "I'd always expected that I'd assume my powers and truly become Devi the Destroyer, or my parents would arrange a marriage for me. Whichever came first, really. But then, pretty much neither seemed to happen, so I decided on a career instead."

A few things occurred to me, the first being: why was it sex *or* a career? But for the time being, it seemed best to focus on the career, which seemed likely to be why she was here.

Even if the sex question was a bit more interesting.

I tried to shift my shoulders to get out an uncomfortable kink, but too much of my back was still granite. I grimaced instead.

Devi rolled her eyes and put her hands on her hips—spreading green goo on that pretty outfit of hers yet again. She didn't seem to notice. "So, to clarify, your issue with my massaging the salve into your muscles is that we don't know each other well enough. And here in the mortal realm we should know each other better first. And massage may or may not imply sex unless I'm a professional. Although I am quite sure not everyone who engages in intercourse knows each other well first. In the meantime, you are in extreme discomfort because part of your body is turned to stone, but you seem to believe I shouldn't massage away your pain until we know each other better. Correct?"

"Yes?" Pretty sure she'd misunderstood at least one of my points somewhere in there.

While her massaging me had relieved some pain, it'd also created a different kind of ache.

I was never going to look at a bad, rock-hard-troll pun the same way again.

"Well…kind of…" I started.

"Can I ask more questions?"

"Um…sure…" Too bad that meant I'd probably have to answer them.

"Do mortals really sacrifice babies to the all-mighty internet and secretly round up gods and goddesses to hunt in a brutal prison-like scenario where the deities are then bashed to death with rocks when they're caught?"

"What? No. We don't do that," I replied quickly,

relieved the first question hadn't been anything personal. Devi seemed to like me so far, didn't seem put off by my size or heritage. I just had to be careful not to put my foot in my mouth.

"Not all the time, but just a sacrifice once a month or so?" Her expression was openly earnest and worried. If she was lying, she was also the finest actress I'd ever met.

"Never. No hurting babies, no bashing anyone with rocks or hunting them. How is it you can be so smart and have studied so much about this realm and yet…think that?"

She shrugged. "It was in the USELESS agent training handbook and required reading."

My chest tightened. "You work for USELESS." Oh, crap. Why had Jenklow gotten me into this?

"Oh, no. I used to, but after the Veils fell, they asked the lead agent to step down, then it was one new manager after another—so many heads rolling. Literally. Very messy."

Hmm… Heimdall had been lead agent. Maybe that explained why he'd called Loki.

Devi shrugged. "That's why I took the buyout package with some others when they decided to clean out most of the staff. Honestly, I wasn't very good at being an agent anyway. Mortals sounded too scary, and I was afraid to go out into the field. Much to my parents' shame."

"If those are the kinds of stories they were spreading about mortals, I'd have been afraid, too," I said slowly. No wonder so many of the agents who came here were so determined to destroy us. I mean, if I thought someone was hunting my kind and murdering babies, I might feel the same way.

But it also made me wonder. If these were some of the

lies spread about us, what were some of the lies that'd been spread about them?

Still, if Devi used to be a USELESS agent but was here with a new job and a new assignment, it was time I knew what.

"Devi, who do you work for now, and what's your assignment?"

"Oh, they're this new group." She cocked her head, her hands pausing on my shoulder. "At least, I think they're new? Only a couple hundred years old or so. That's still new, isn't it? Anyway, they're called the Guardians. And my mission is easy. I'm just supposed to make sure Beckwell can't hurt us. All it will take is one little bomb."

Chapter Three

MY BRAIN STUTTERED like I was having a stroke following Devi's pronouncement. One little bomb. My town. Death and destruction. When my brain rebooted, it was going to be in panic mode. Hell, maybe I was already there. My breath grew rough and uneven. I wasn't the hero-type. I didn't know how to handle bomb threats. I was an officer administrator, an ex-biker. I'd much rather be gardening, or out on a ride on Edith, or, or…

Mr. Whiskers jumped down with a small meow, curling around my ankle and looking up at me as though telling me to just breathe and calm the flip down.

"Um… I said something wrong, didn't I?" Devi said quietly. Her hands paused where she worked them in tandem down my shoulder blades, making me bite back a groan.

"No! I mean, nope, no problem. No problem." Bad idea to piss off a destruction goddess. "I mean, uh… I'm sure you'll make a great field agent. What, um, what kind of bomb are we talking here? You just caught me a bit by surprise, that's all."

All I could picture was my town as a smoking crater. All the people I knew and cared about—my dad, Mr. Whiskers—all of them burned up and gone. Or possibly worse, suffering. My head started to pound. I had to get Devi to the Senior Center, pronto. It was long past time that I handed this problem over to the proper authorities.

"Well, it's not supposed to destroy Beckwell. Or at least, only a little bit of it. Frizzly, you're making me nervous. Please, tell me what I'm supposed to say to make this better." Her fingers worked deep into the muscle tissue of my neck and shoulders. Then working lower, down my spine, the salve making her hands and my flesh slick and slippery, which did nothing to help my muddled brain.

"I… I don't know what you're supposed to say." I should have. I dealt with pissed-off minotaurs, impatient imps, and sourpuss sorcerers in my job as a medical assistant on an almost daily basis. Then there were the Beckwell seniors. Even when I'd just worked maintenance at the Center, I'd known how to deal with residents, what to say, how to calm them down, what the next move was. But with Devi, facing the destruction of my entire town, my home, the one place I'd almost belonged… I was a troll and I sure the hell was no match for a goddess.

"You seem upset, and even the places where you're not stone, your muscles are tense." Her hands delved lower, to my lower back. Her chin almost rested on the back of my neck. Her breath ruffled the hair on my nape. Fabric rustled as she stood then came around front of me.

My brain stuttered again as she once more stepped between my knees and knelt.

She looked up at me, her hair brushing my thighs that were no longer stone and felt her every touch with pinprick intensity. So far as distractions went, this was a really, *really* good one.

"Maybe there's some way I can make you feel better." She scooped up a dollop of green goop and smoothed it down my shoulder and over my left nipple.

Wait. Had it been stone there? The touch of her fingertips burned through me, and it'd been my back that took most of the sun.

I knew she was a destruction goddess and everything, but when she smiled up at me like that, like I'd cleared away the clouds and made the stars come out, it made me feel like I was ten feet tall and a superhero. I'd do just about anything to make her smile at me that way again.

It was entirely possible the rock had petrified my brain.

Beckwell. Destruction. Fate of everyone you care about. I fought for focus. Real heroes would have been able to ignore all this. I mean, they were probably more used to women touching them anyway and would find a way to ignore… Oh, gods. Her hands felt so good… Dammit!

"Uh, if you really want to help, not destroying everything would be great." My voice was rough and raspy.

She slid her hands down over my other nipple, then down my chest, smoothing over my belly that had gone rock hard without any actual granite involved. Her dark gaze locked with mine. "Yes, I can see why you might say that. If I was the real Devi, I could just destroy all of Beckwell with a thought. That would certainly make my parents proud. But since I'm not, just a little destruction is going to have to do. It's only to protect my new employers, you see. They said there are dangerous people here, people who want to destroy them."

The towel wasn't going to cut it much longer to hide the effect of her touch, and my tongue had thickened inside my mouth. My brain focused only on her touch and her lips and the way her breasts brushed my arms as she worked over me.

She dipped her hands in the goop once more and reached for my chest.

I bit back a groan and tried to focus on her face. "Devi, this is my home. Yeah, people coming to try and destroy us is kind of common. I try not to take it personally, but… I work every day at the Senior Center in the med clinic. I know every Beckwell citizen, including a lot of the new ones because when they need help, they come to us. Those I don't know through my job I know through my dad, who's completely human but a math teacher over at the school. They're good people. Innocent people…well, mostly." I dragged a hand over my jaw to refocus. Just too many damn things going on around my chest, in my brain, and under my towel. "They're good people; that's the point. Even if a few have done…er, questionable things. They're *my* people"

She frowned. "I thought you didn't take threats to your town personally."

"I said I tried not to." I couldn't stifle the next groan. Was I the only one affected by this? Maybe she was just messing with me. A distraction before she destroyed everything…although there were worse ways to die.

Her breath ruffled the hair on my leg, and she made a small sound, almost a small moan. "It's just a job, Frizzly." Her hands reached for the edge of my towel. "I don't really want to hurt anyone. I don't think anyone will feel anything. The bomb is just supposed to stop residents from using their abilities against us." She began to slide her hands beneath my towel.

I jumped up from the chair, not a trace of rock left other than the organic bit from her touch. "I can't. I… I'm going to go put on some clothes." I ran out of the living room and across the hall to my bedroom, then slammed the door.

I leaned against the closed door like a flipping coward. Shit, shit, shit. Why had those old Shades bastards put me in this position? Bad enough that every day at work I had to listen to their old war stories about saving the world from tyranny back in the day. Protecting Beckwell was supposed to be *their* job, not mine. I was no hero. A real hero would have maybe seduced Devi out of her plan, not run away. No wonder Mr. Whiskers had a better love life than I did.

I made sure the door was locked—not sure if they had those where Devi was from, or if she'd be bold enough to follow me in, or what exactly my plan was if she did—but I had to start thinking about my town and why she was here and what I was going to do about it. Not just about how good her touch felt, how sweet her smile was, and how she made warmth flow through me in a way I'd never felt before. As though I were something special. I snorted. Even my own mother hadn't wanted me.

All through school, everyone seemed to fit in, find their place in a way I never had. I'd wondered if it was the troll side of me people saw, some part of me that was unlikeable, too drawn to violence. After a while, it'd been too easy to fall into that role. When I was with the bikers, I was the one you picked a fight with since I was the biggest. Trouble was, soon I couldn't look at myself in the mirror. Didn't think even Dad could be proud of me anymore. I couldn't be that person again. Not for Devi, not even for Beckwell.

I strode across the small bedroom toward the en suite, clenching and unclenching my hands, trying to figure out this game and what I was missing. I grabbed the towel off the rack, dropping the one I'd been wearing all this time, and brusquely wiped myself down as much as I could reach, removing the residue of green goo.

I always seemed to be missing something. I might not be an idiot, even if I was doing a damned good impression of one today. Especially when it came to women, or being anything other than my normal, boring self. Maybe this was all some game by Devi, pretending to be all big-eyed and innocent, rescuing my cat, whipping up that salve and smoothing it into every inch of my skin…even if it'd seemed pretty plausible at the time.

I chucked both towels into the hamper, then stalked back out into the room, systematically grabbing clothes and dragging them on, distracted. Hell, I'd been running around mostly naked for how long now? Shorts. Socks. Jeans. Shirt. I glanced a moment in the mirror at the rumpled short red spikes and my close-cropped beard, which, on the doc's wife's advice, I'd trimmed square to follow my jawline last week. But I didn't spare more than a glance at the mirror since I knew what would stare back. A guy who was more big than anything else, including attractive or interesting. Until I'd met Devi, I'd been okay with a small, predictable life.

It hadn't much mattered that I wasn't more interesting.

Shit. Like it had ever really mattered. I glared at the idiot in the mirror. I was just the mark. Although, it still didn't make sense that Devi had ended up here.

There was a timid knock on my door. "Frizzly? Are you all right?" Devi called, her voice more subdued than I'd heard it other than when she'd talked about her family not approving of her. Her family sounded like a bunch of useless tits.

"Yeah. Fine," I said, dragging a brush through my hair a couple of times.

"I… You're angry because I said I'm here to destroy the town, aren't you? Or…well, is it because I touched you like that? I shouldn't have done that, either." A pause. "I, um…you weren't stone on your chest. I just…the way you look at me is so different than anyone I've ever met before, and your body is so beautiful and…" She cleared her throat, her voice seeming to shrink with every word. "I'm sorry."

I put down my brush and blew out a breath, hanging my head. "Devi? Why the hell are you at my house anyway? Why did you rescue Mr. Whiskers and then make that salve for me?"

There was a long pause, then finally her voice, still timid and small. "I, uh, got lost," she almost whispered. She gave a sad laugh. "'Typical Devi,' Mother and Father would say. My first real assignment for the new boss, and I got lost on the way there. The end of the portal didn't open where I expected. There was some kind of…interference that brought me here instead. I was trying to figure out which way to go out of the forest when I saw your cat—I'd only read about felines before. Then you seemed in distress, and I wanted to help." There was another long pause. "You probably want me to leave now, don't you?"

I was finally getting more information from her with the door closed, and undoubtedly because her hands were no longer against my naked flesh. But I was also raw and tired of being jerked around by her, Jenklow, and the others. Hell, even the bloody eagle and Mr. Whiskers. I yanked open the door with more force than I'd intended.

She tumbled into me with a small cry.

I caught her but very quickly put some distance between us, crossing my arms so I wasn't tempted to touch her. "Is this a game to you?"

She straightened, craning her neck slightly to meet my gaze. "A game? A quaint passing of time, like cards or Monopoly?"

"No. A game. Trying to trick me, confuse me, make me do stupid things." Think stupid things. Feel stupid things.

She swallowed and shook her head, twisting her hands in front of her. "No. I-I didn't want to do that. I really did just get lost after I dropped out of the reality bubble." She dropped her gaze. "Although…I did want to touch you. I shouldn't have taken advantage of you. A mere mortal."

Her head only came to the middle of my chest, she'd just spent I wasn't sure how long massaging my body with her bare hands, and just when I'd really needed her, she'd run in and rescued Mr. Whiskers. Yet she was afraid *she* was taking advantage of *me*?

"I…don't think that was the case," I said, hating the slump in her shoulders, the way she seemed to shrink into herself, nervously twining her hands and her fingers together. I leaned down closer to her. "I…liked you touching me. Which was why I had to leave. And put on some clothes. I wasn't sure if, well, that is…"

Her head popped up, expression brightening. "You wanted to have sexual intercourse with me? You thought me attractive or interesting, perhaps?"

I glommed onto the last comment, because no way was I touching the first. "Devi, you're one of the most beautiful females—woman, goddess, unicorn—that I've ever seen. I've never met anyone quite like you."

Her lips curved upward, broader and broader, and all the stars and light in the universe came out to play in her expression. "Really? You're not just saying that because you don't want me to destroy your town?"

"No, I don't want you to destroy Beckwell… But I'm not just saying it because I think you want to hear it, either."

If I'd ever dared dream of the perfect woman for me, she'd have been it.

Too damned bad we were already doomed.

She glowed again, and the urge to give her flowers and curl my body around hers to protect her surged through me.

Unfortunately, eight-hundred-and-some lives said I had to turn her over to Jenklow, the Four, and whoever would make sure she couldn't hurt any one of those Beckwellians. The sooner she was out of my house, the better. I'd get back to my life, and she…she wouldn't be allowed to hurt anyone. Which meant I had to get her to the Senior Center without triggering her suspicions.

She was curious about new experiences here. I could show her one of my favorite pastimes *and* get her to the Center. Plus, the fact that I'd be able to give her back something in return for her kindness soothed the growing ache inside me that said once she was turned over to Jenklow and the others, once real heroes had their say, I'd probably never see Devi again.

"Say, would you like to meet Edith?"

Her eyes narrowed, and she took a step back from me, back stiffening. "Your wife? The one responsible for the beautiful flowers out front?"

"What? No. Those are my flowers. I like gardening." My face heated. "Edith is my bike—motorcycle." It was official. I was the most pathetic resident of Beckwell.

"Motorcycle…" I could tell Devi was once again attempting to match the term with whatever the hell she knew about my world.

When had it become my world and her world? It was just one world now. If the stories were true, that's how it had been in the beginning, before it'd been split off between the different species. Except here in Beckwell, even when we kept talking about how we were all equal, even among the magical species we continued to fight.

Gods versus us, everyone pissing on demons, the Shades manipulating me into dealing with a potentially dangerous destruction goddess and almost murdering my cat in the process.

I kept talking even while I worked out the rest of the plan. "Edith, my bike, is a kind of vehicle. Only two wheels, gets you from place to place with way more fun and style than a car. I'm guessing they don't have those where you come from?" My limited experience with women pointed to the fact that Edith was by far the most interesting and coolest thing about me.

"Oh, a motorcycle. I've heard of those! Motorized versions of the two-wheeled bicycle contraption," Devi said, her expression again brightening with a smile that lifted those full, lush lips, crinkled the skin around eyes that twinkled and glowed brighter than the moon.

My insides squeezed with guilt. Either she was a brilliant actress…or I was about to turn a sweet, semi-destruction goddess over to those I doubted would be as sympathetic to her need to please her family or see that there had to be something redeeming about someone who would save a strange cat and even stranger troll. Was there some possible way I could save Beckwell *and* Devi? Maybe if I changed her mind about the "little" bomb, or whatever it was she really had planned. Was there such a thing as a small bomb when you were a destruction goddess? Or the granddaughter of one? Well, I might not be a hero, but I was good at talking. Maybe I could make the Shades see that Devi wasn't so bad. She was just…a little lost.

I forced a smile. "Just let me gear up to go outside, then let's go meet Edith."

She took a deep breath, then nodded solemnly, hands clenched and arms stiff at her sides. "Yes, that's probably for the best." The bubbly energy had drained from Devi's voice.

A lump settled in the pit of my stomach, like I'd been half-turned to stone all over again as I returned to my bedroom to gear up with 400SPF. I was trying to follow Dad's rules: Be kind and honest, not get involved. Sucked that I didn't know if I was making the right decision, even as I texted Jenklow and the others to tell them we were on our way. "Maybe…maybe I can introduce you to some friends. People who could help us find a compromise where you don't lose your job, but you don't destroy Beckwell, either."

Devi made a face. "I'm not sure that's possible. The parameters of the mission are quite clear…" She shrugged. "But maybe we can try."

Damn straight we could. Had to. Jenklow and the rest of the cagey old paranormal warriors that made up the Shades had gotten me into this dangerous mess. Now I had to trust that they could get me—and maybe Devi—out of it, too. Hopefully, without anyone exploding.

Chapter Four

MY STOMACH CONTINUED to twist as we pulled into the Senior Center parking lot with a crunch of gravel and Devi's enthusiastic whoops. I cut Edith's engine, the silence filled with the hum of insects and birds from the woods behind the circular single-story modern building. I turned and couldn't help but mirror Devi's wide, slightly dazed smile. It was enough to make me almost forget, momentarily, that we were about to put ourselves at the mercy of wily Beckwell senior citizens. It's what had to be done. If Devi was here to harm any part of Beckwell, I had to stop her. Or rather, get her to people who could.

"That was…fabulous!" Devi cried. "There was nothing in the information I read about the rumble and the noise and the speed and the wind and the…" She blew out a breath in rapture, face glowing as she looked up from beneath my helmet. Her words made me remember the first time I'd gotten onto a bike. The freedom and lightness of that experience, at one with my world for the first time in my life.

I hadn't bothered with a helmet, seeing as how I was

more likely to dent the road than the other way around. It'd been more important to slather on the 400SPF concoction Cara brewed me because as much as I wouldn't mind Devi smoothing her salve onto my flesh again, as a rock I was useless to Beckwell.

She took my offered hand and stepped off the bike first, staring all around like we were in the most interesting place she'd ever been.

I tried to see the familiar from her perspective. The modern, multi-windowed circular Senior Center was the most contemporary building in Beckwell, and a sight I saw almost daily. It was expansive and welcoming, with large windows and glass-enclosed entrances. Cheerful, brightly colored flowers climbed the taupe walls and spilled out of their pots along the sidewalk, giving it a friendly, welcoming homeyness. I wasn't responsible for all the yard upkeep anymore, but I still lent a hand now and then, felt that swell of pride to see it looking good.

"It's so fortunate you have powerful friends who will help us. I was terrified we'd have to meet those murderous horsewomen." She shuddered. "I don't understand why they'd want to destroy all of existence just for fun." Devi turned that full-wattage smile on me as she stepped to my side.

I forgot all about the flowers, the horsewomen and the Shades, hell, even forgot my name for a second or two, and offered my hand to her. I blinked, trying to regain focus. "Er, the Four don't want to destroy anything." So long as they and Beckwell weren't under threat, but I left that part out. "I'm not exactly certain what these, um, friends will suggest." Hopefully, I wouldn't have to get between them and Devi. My insides churned more. I took a deep, steadying breath and forced a smile. "But whatever happens, we'll do it together, all right?"

Her small fingers closed around mine, but there was a moment of hesitation before her gaze met mine, a moment longer before her smile that was shadowed with something else. "Whatever happens, thank you for the time we've had together. I'll always be grateful I was able to rescue Mr. Whiskers. Because it meant I met you."

At the touch of our fingers there was that momentary zing and tingle between us. She'd saved my cat this morning, and if I were honest, me, since the sun had been more intense than I'd expected. Gods knew how long I'd have been out there, a garden statue, until someone… My insides twisted. It'd probably have been Dad who'd have found me, petrified, possibly for good. After everything he'd done for me, I could never do that to him.

My gaze turned to Devi's dark head. She'd been kind to me, whatever her end motives. Dad's advice came back to me: When in doubt, kindness and honesty were always the right policy. I'd made a lot of mistakes in my life not following that advice. The Shades knew she was coming. This was probably a trap, and I was about to lead the one woman I'd met who made me feel like I could be…more, right into it.

I'd never wanted to be a hero. Maybe, like Devi, I'd always just wanted people to look at me and see me, not just the troll. I wanted to help my town, but I didn't want to do it at the cost of someone else's life. Didn't want to become a man that Dad—or I—couldn't be proud of.

Just before we reached the entrance, I tugged her to the side, out of view of the glass doors, and turned her toward me. It was our last chance before we met Jenklow and the rest of the Shades, along with whoever the hell else might be inside, waiting for us. Waiting for her.

"Devi, do you *want* to destroy Beckwell?" I said, voice urgent.

Her long pause and the distant look in her eyes drove a stabbing pain through me as bad or worse than being turned to stone. Her fingers squeezed around mine, and she bit her lip a moment and took a breath before she spoke. "Do you know what it's like to live your entire life and never be enough?" she said quietly.

Images from my school years, when I'd never quite fit in, even among other magical descendants, flashed through my head. Then my years with the biker gang, the gnomes and Norms, both of which had always seen me as something outside of them. Dad had always been proud… at least he'd said he was. But for someone, just once, to look at me and recognize I was worth more than just being big and tough?

"Yeah, I do," I said honestly. "But, Devi, if this is about your parents, do you think they'll ever—"

She reached up and touched a finger to my lips, silencing me. Her smile was sad. "From the way you talk about your father, I can tell that whatever you've done, whoever you'll be, he's proud of you. That's all I want Frizzly. But… I was given a destruction goddess' name, and I've never actually destroyed anything. No matter how hard I practice, no matter how hard I try…" Her shoulders slumped. "The best I've managed was turning my paperwork to dust, and I'm not quite sure what happened to my coworker's salamander. I'm not half-bad with transmutation, even if my results are inconsistent at best. It's why I didn't try to turn you back into a man that way. Look at that eagle I saved Mr. Whiskers from. I was trying to turn him into a fish."

I resisted asking why she'd wanted to turn the eagle into a fish. "Not being good at destroying things sounds like a *good* thing. Especially if it means you won't destroy my town. Devi, whatever you're planning, you can't do this. You can't harm Beckwell. Please."

She slowly tugged her hand from mine. "I'm sorry. I…I thought you might understand. This is my chance. My *one* chance. I have to take it. Besides, like I say, my boss promised it was just to protect us. I'm sorry." She'd barely finished speaking before she lifted her hand, and there was a bright flare of light.

The flash momentarily blinded me. I flailed blindly a few moments.

I suspect it was meant to do more than that, and maybe she'd forgotten what I'd told her about trolls: one of our primary abilities is being pretty much immune to magic. Rocks are like that. My vision cleared to catch the swish of the double glass sliding doors closing, and a flash of Devi's sapphire scarf.

"Shit." I raced toward the doors.

Flashes of brilliant light lit up the central atrium of the Senior Center. What the hell?

Men shouted inside.

Someone else, maybe Devi, shouted back.

Between more mini explosions of light, puffs of smoke, and more shouting, I struggled to spot Devi and identify anyone else. What I should have done was back the hell out of there and run, back to Mr. Whiskers, back to my house and petunias.

But…this was the Senior Center. Devi was in danger. Other residents might be caught in the crossfire, too.

In one of my dumber moves for the day—and, yeah, I'd already made a few—I lowered my head and charged into the airy high-ceiling atrium of the Senior Center and the current battlefield. My heart pounded, and the smoke burned my eyes, blurred my vision. The collection of sofas and tables usually gathered near the center of the room had been tossed about, some of them tipped on their sides. Thank the gods, no residents meandered through on their walkers nor stood on the sidelines to place bets on the winner like a lot of the atrium firefights.

Happened more than you'd expect in a place like this.

Crouched behind one flowered sofa was the offensive team, probably the Shades. Occasionally, a wrinkled hand would lob a fireball, or another would lift a cane that shot out a shower of sparks and magic. Another resident lobbed what appeared to be a magical grenade, judging from the way the glowing orb exploded in rainbow hues.

I growled, rushing toward Devi behind another overturned sofa and crouching down beside her. The odd fireball and attack orb bounced off my shoulders, probably toasting my clothes, but they were just clothes, and the attacks didn't feel much different to me than getting hit with tennis balls. This was the worst firefight I'd seen in the atrium in a year. Beckwell Seniors meant those sofas were occasionally incinerated. One of them was already smoldering.

Devi was crunched into a small ball, hiding behind the bulk of an overturned sofa. She turned and looked at me, eyes wide, soot staining her cheeks and most of her hair coming out of its bun and hanging around her shoulders. Clutched in her hand was a glowing golden orb, like a transparent fist-sized pearl with gold and shimmering gas whirling inside. "I have to do this. I have to prove I'm not useless, that I'm worthy of my name."

"That's a bomb in her hand, Frizzly. Take it from her or get out of the way," an old man shouted from behind one of the sofas. It might have been Mr. Jenklow.

Damn, damn, damn. Why had they attacked her instead of talking first?

My gaze went to that shimmering, apparently deadly

orb Devi gripped. I gulped, dropping to my knees next to her and cupping her hand and the orb in my big mitts. "I can't let you do this," I said. We trolls could survive a lot of things. Pretty sure a bomb of any kind wasn't one of them. But my hands didn't move from her trembling grip and the warm orb.

Her wide eyes were wet and shining. "What else can I do? You weren't supposed to be here. I knew you'd try to stop me, so I tried a stun-spell outside. I forgot you're immune to magic. You were supposed to sleep through this."

My shoulders sagged. "And you thought that'd somehow make it okay?"

"We didn't break our word," another of the Shades called across the atrium. "She came in with the bomb in her hand. We had to do something."

"Do you have the bomb yet? My knees can't take much more of this," still another shouted.

I massaged my throbbing forehead. So much for not getting involved. I focused on Devi, tried to keep my voice even. She'd tried to knock me out in the parking lot, then come in here, ready to place the bomb. Awesome-sauce. "You pulled out the bomb as soon as you got inside," I said quietly to Devi. It wasn't a question. That explained why the Shades decided to shoot first.

"Of course! My bosses told me this place, these people were dangerous. You don't understand, Frizzly. They'd have killed me otherwise. It was my only chance."

"You didn't try to blow me up when we met, and I live here. And the source of this information, the ones saying we were dangerous, don't suppose those are the same bosses who told you we sacrificed babies to internet gods?" I couldn't prevent the hit of sarcasm in my tone, even though it jabbed me in the soft bits, the way she winced and scooched away from me, the flash of pain and betrayal in her dark gaze. Hurt or not, I didn't loosen my grip covering her hands and the bomb. Gods, I hated how people always seemed ready to believe the worst about another person, another group. What the hell happened to the truth or benefit of the doubt?

"You told them we were coming. I did what I thought was best," she said stiffly.

I growled, the orb growing warmer between our fingers. "So did I. They said they could talk to you, do the hero thing and convince you not to destroy our town. What the hell was I supposed to do, Devi? I don't know you." The words had the sour taste of a lie because meeting her was like meeting a part of myself I'd never even known was missing. Made me hope, wonder if this so-called life plan of mine might be a little too safe, a little too lonely.

I hadn't given her the benefit of the doubt, either. Had seen her kindness as a ploy, instead of just…kindness.

"Let go of me," she bit out, the orb between us growing hotter, the gold flickering to red that glowed between my fingers. An answering red glow flared in Devi's dark eyes, like twin flames.

Yeah, I must have misplaced my brain somewhere this morning. Either that, or it was still a chunk of granite. Because now I was also pissing off a destruction goddess. Who was holding a bomb.

"Frizzly? How's it going out there, son?" Jenklow called again.

"I'm kinda busy," I shouted back, my gaze never leaving Devi's. I hated being judged for my ancestry, for my size. I'd judged Devi for the same. She deserved the benefit of the doubt just the same as anyone else. Yeah, fine, she really had come here to destroy Beckwell, but I was certain that wasn't who she really was. Was betting my life on it.

"Don't do this." I leaned closer to her, over our hands clasped around that freaking bomb. "Devi, whatever the hell they told you, what do you think happens when a *destruction goddess* sets off a bomb? Their mission, your parents' approval, that isn't worth your life. You think things are still going to be small and simple? That the explosion 'won't really hurt anyone'?

She blinked, the red hue in her gaze dimming a little, the orb cooling slightly against my fingers. "I… But I'm not a real destruction goddess." She looked down at her hands. "And it doesn't look like a real bomb. I mean, not a mortal world one. I read about those once, too, how mortals have done terrible things to each other with them."

"So you built this yourself? You know exactly how it works?"

"Well…" Her shoulders shrank in on her. "I don't know how to build a bomb. But they told me—"

"How long have you worked for them? Are you certain you can trust them?" The weight of the next words stuck to my tongue for a moment because I knew they'd hit home. Dad's voice in my head warned me not to do it, but Beckwell was at stake. Benefit of the doubt or not, saving the town wasn't just playing nice. "Have you proved how valuable you are to them? How worthy?"

She flinched like I'd struck her, and I felt like the biggest asshole this side of Mexico. The red hue faded completely from her dark gaze, her shoulders sagged even further, and her hands began to shake harder under mine. Her voice when she spoke was barely a whisper. "But… they promised." Unshed tears swam in her eyes as her gaze met mine. "This is supposed to be my chance. My sister introduced me to them. This is supposed to be how I make my family proud."

"And you're willing to gamble that people you don't know very well, that care nothing about you or about anyone who lives in this town, have told you the truth?"

"I…don't know."

"Hey, Jenklow, and any of the rest of you over there," I said, raising my voice to a shout to be heard across the atrium by the people lobbing fireballs at us. "Anyone over there know what happens if a destruction goddess sets off a magical bomb?"

"What kind of bomb?" This gruff voice was from Mr. Liko, Beckwell's former chief of police, who was also probably figuring out how to somehow rappel off a wall and land on top of us. Didn't seem to matter how many times he broke a hip.

"Knock it off, Liko!" grumbled another of the voices. Possibly Mr. Einar, otherwise known as Old Henry. He and Mr. Jenklow were rarely found far from each other.

The smoldering sofa burst into red-hot flame.

Another projectile, a water-orb apparently, bounced off me and then hit the sofa, dousing the fire. These poor sofas were never going to be the same. These ones had only lasted three months since the last firefight in the atrium.

"Actually," came a thin, reedy voice that sounded like it belonged to a scared teenager. That made it Mr. Zaki, who'd looked like he'd barely turned twenty-one my entire life. He didn't talk much but was undoubtedly the smartest of the bunch. "If she's a destruction goddess—"

"I'm not actually. My grandmother is. Or, well, kind of grandmother," Devi added.

This resulted in more half-whispered discussion. Only half-whispered, because someone's hearing aids had obviously gone dead, which meant most of it had to be repeated twice for whoever that was.

"Regardless—" it was Zaki again, "—destruction goddess or descendant of one, the explosion will feed the destruction urge within you. For want of a better term, it's a trigger. The bomb will explode, then your genes will demand more and more destruction…until you probably explode, too."

Devi turned to me, eyes wide, voice strangled. "He's lying. He has to be lying."

"He's not lying," Mr. Jenklow shouted. "That's what Heimdall warned Loki about after he left USELESS. Said you had a lot of potential, and that all your power could be used against you. This isn't worth your life, Ms. Devi."

"And we're running short of time. Either we end this here, or you surrender, Ms. Devi," Mr. Einar said. "Because if I calculate correctly, we have a short time before someone calls in the back-up orderlies, then they'll call the police chief, who might call the Four and Loki. Unless you'd like to continue the conversation with them, perhaps we could retire somewhere more comfortable."

"Frizzly, son, for the last time, can you get that bomb away from Ms. Devi, please? And do handle it carefully," Mr. Jenklow added, seamlessly picking up from where Mr. Einar left off. They were almost like an old married couple…the kind who still liked each other.

I turned again to Devi. "So? What's it going to be? Because you don't strike me as the kind of person who wants to kill a whole bunch of people, including yourself."

"You said you didn't know anything about me," she whispered.

I leaned down until our foreheads touched. "I might have lied about that part," I whispered. "You have been nothing but kind since we've met. Heimdall was right. You have a lot of potential to be whatever you want to be, but you'll never figure out what that is if you keep following other people's visions. Come on, Devi. Please. Give me the bomb. Don't do this."

Her fingers trembled more around the explosive orb, which had settled back down to the shimmering gold.

I held my breath for one count… Two…

At last, she nodded slowly and pulled her hands out from mine, leaving me cradling the explosive. Which suddenly seemed more explosive. This was so not the day I'd pictured last night when I'd gone to bed. I couldn't take my eyes off the shimmering death cradled in my hands. Oh gods, what if I squeezed too hard, or tripped, or—

"Put your hands in the air and slowly come out from behind the sofa," Liko said, all police chief again, which only made my neck tighten.

I'd been in a gang too long to ever forget the way a policeman demanding you put your hands in the air was never a good thing. "If I put my hands in the air, I'm likely to drop this."

"Liko, stop being an ass. She surrendered, Frizzly has the bomb," Mr. Einar scolded the former policeman.

"But—" Liko started.

"But you heard him. Stop being an ass. If that's even possible," the fifth of their group said, sounding smug as usual. Typical Mr. Chaimek.

"I need your word that you won't harm Devi," I called back, my gaze lifting to meet Devi's. "She might have intended harm, but she was manipulated and tricked. She didn't hurt anyone in the end. That has to count for something."

There was a rapid discussion.

Mr. Jenklow spoke up before the discussion was complete. "You have my word, Frizzly. Neither you nor

Ms. Devi will be harmed. We just want to speak with you. And, of course, we couldn't let the Center or our town come to harm."

"Now on your feet," Liko barked.

"You first," I shouted back, but I was only buying us a few minutes, my gaze again coming to the shimmering orb. At this point, we didn't have much choice other than to trust the old men.

Gods help us.

I turned to Devi, dropping my voice so only she could hear me. "I'm going to stand first, then you stand. Make sure I'm between you and them. Got it?"

She nodded, the tiniest of movements. "Why are you helping me?"

I gave her a small smile. "Because you saved my cat. Because you deserve to have someone believe in you. And because I don't want to see anyone get hurt today." I gave her a nod, then clambered to my feet. Not my smoothest move but, seeing as I didn't want to risk falling on or dropping the explosive, it'd have to do.

Devi climbed lithely to her feet, and together we faced the group who'd caused mayhem in the Senior Center Atrium…again.

Five old men faced us. Mr. Jenklow, with bright blue eyes, a cane, almost completely bald with bushy white eyebrows gave me a smile and a nod that I didn't know how to interpret. Beside him stood Mr. Einar, proud and still straight, with a shock of white hair and a harder blue gaze. Mr. Chaimek, handsome with a salt-and-pepper moustache, hefted a bag onto his shoulder that I surmised must have held some of the things they'd been throwing at us, while potbellied Mr. Liko, light-brown bald head shining with sweat, gave us a thin-lipped glare. Last was Mr. Zaki, who pushed his glasses up his narrow nose, his hair a black mop on his head, prominent Adam's apple bobbing. These were the Shades, huh?

I blew out a breath, finally able to take a better look around, what with magic and fireballs not flying through the air. The front desk near the far wall and the doors to the dining hall sat suspiciously empty. The Med Clinic's glass windows to the right lay dark. No sign of residents, orderlies, or attendants coming running to restore order.

Whatever they'd expected when I said Devi and I were on the way, the Shades had planned this out carefully.

I glanced at Devi, who stole a look up at me before hiding slightly behind me, her hand on my elbow. "It's them…or we'll probably be dealing with the Four," I said quietly.

She visibly shuddered.

Considering what she'd been told about mortals, I could only imagine what worse things she'd heard about the Four. Not that I especially wanted to deal with them myself. They weren't the monsters Devi probably believed. Sure, War and Death could be a bit…intense, but Famine's muffins were the tastiest thing I'd ever eaten, and Pestilence was my boss' wife and someone I considered close to a friend. Still…we couldn't be certain which side they'd fall on the Devi issue. Now that they oversaw protecting and running Beckwell, which had expanded significantly with the rise of magic throughout the mortal world, they took a dim view to anyone threatening to destroy us.

"I say we trust the Shades," she whispered back. "They seem like they'll keep their word. I hope."

I nodded since that's what I'd decided…before the fire fight in the atrium. Finally, people who knew how to deal with this sort of problem—people coming to try and destroy Beckwell, how to stop them, how to suss out information, all of it—finally they'd be in charge, not me.

Mr. Einar gave us a wave and pointed down the hall, indicating we follow him, all of us leaving the mess behind us for someone else to deal with. It looked like Albert Jenklow, Henry Einar, and the other old sneaks really were our best chance. Hell. We had little other choice but to hurry after him, and hope we'd made the right gamble.

Chapter Five

THE FACT that the halls were so empty made my neck twitch. It was almost snack time—there should have been residents all over the place, plus lined up outside the dining hall. Yet instead, as we followed Mr. Einar down the hall toward what I'm pretty sure was Mr. Jenklow's suite, other than the few faces that peered out at us from their doorways, there was no one. I couldn't remember the halls being so quiet since the battle of the Four when USELESS had sent another goddess to destroy Beckwell.

Things hadn't turned out well for that goddess. She'd ended up confined for eternity in a ketchup bottle. None of which made me feel better about deciding to trust the Shades. If things went bad, if they decided to break their word to leave Devi unharmed, was there anything I could do about it? This was supposed to be what I'd wanted: someone else to take over, someone else to put on the cape and tights and let me get back to trying to be kind and keeping my head down.

My gaze slid sideways. And yet…

Devi walked beside me like she was headed for the

gallows, her arms wrapped around herself, shoulders hunched, and avoiding my gaze. Her usually warm brown skin was an unhealthy chalky gray.

I wanted to reassure her, but what would be the point? She had come to cause harm. Although she hadn't believed she'd actually destroy Beckwell, and in the end, she'd decided against causing any harm. Someone had to make sure she got a fair shake, which was the only reason I'd stuck around. Still, my stomach twisted again. More so when we reached the mauve door labeled with the name plate "Jenklow."

Mr. Liko stood outside it, arms crossed, thin moustache twitching. Age may have substituted some of his muscle for belly, but he still bore the imposing bearing I imagined he'd employed when he'd been Beckwell's police chief. Hell, who was I kidding? He still intimidated the hell out of me, even if I was more than a foot and a half taller. Way I heard it, he'd once taken down a gang of magic-deniers by himself, with only a wooden spoon.

He gave me a disdainful sniff, his black gaze flicking over me before he turned his glower on Devi. Not that she noticed, the way she studied the tiled floor.

Liko held the door while Devi slipped inside the room, followed by myself, Mr. Einar, and finally, Mr. Liko.

It was a standard bachelor suite that faced the wild area behind the Center, lush green leaves and grass beckoning and hinting at freedom just beyond reach of the broad windows. A simple kitchenette and bistro table was off to the far left, then space for the single bed and dresser. The seating area lay directly in front of us and the door. Two aging floral sofas faced each other, Mr. Zaki hunched on one of them, hands clasped between his bony knees. Mr. Einar took a seat near the end of the other one, across from Mr. Jenklow, who's bright blue gaze and smile were almost welcoming…and definitely scheming.

Mr. Liko grunted, taking his place on this side of the door, arms crossed, and I tried not to twitch, what with him behind my back.

"Are you sure none of those blasts hurt you, Mr. Frizzly?" Mr. Chaimek inquired, a charming rascal I knew for a fact had attempted to "liberate" the Center's pharmacy of its contents at least twice. He sounded more curious that I was unaffected than concerned.

I should have been asking when I could get out of here and back to work, doing my job instead of theirs, but for some reason that wasn't what came out of my mouth. "I'm fine. So, which one of you tried to kill my cat, and what exactly are your intentions when it comes to Ms. Devi?"

"I'm sure your cat was never in any real danger," Mr. Einar said, silver elf-tongue of his charming as always. "But we needed to make sure that you and Ms. Devi met. Chaimek set up the field to make sure she came through the portal on your property rather than closer to the Senior Center. Wouldn't you know it, but your property is aligned with the ley lines, giving it something of a magnetic pull when it comes to portals. Of course, this means you should probably be on the alert for other unexpected arrivals, too. Although that's another reason it made sense to divert arrivals to you. As a troll, you're less susceptible to magic."

"So that's why I got lost. I don't usually have so much trouble with portals," Devi murmured.

"You are as lovely and with as great a potential or more than Heimdall suggested," Mr. Chaimek said, giving Devi a wink.

I, however, found heat climbing my face, and red clouded my vision. "Oh, I see. So not only did you try to kill Mr. Whiskers, but you were also fine with sacrificing me, too?"

Mr. Chaimek scoffed. "Hardly. We were almost certain your troll genes would hold up against any magic she could throw at you. Besides, being part basilisk, one of the worst things she could do was turn you to stone. Thanks to that beast of yours, that's hardly out of the norm, is it?"

"Heimdall used to be my boss at USELESS. He knew I'd be coming?" Devi asked. Her face colored. "He knew I'd be foolish enough to agree to a plan that would get myself and others killed?" She shook her head, voice breaking. "Seems like I just had potential for stupidity and harm."

"Oh, now, it's not that bad," Mr. Jenklow said, patting her knee and looking desperately to the others to back him up. "Right, boys?"

"Not at all bad," Mr. Einar agreed more smoothly. "He obviously thought you had power."

"And didn't know anything about us, the mortal world or those abilities," Mr. Liko said bluntly, earning a glare from me and the rest of the Shades. He snorted and shrugged. "What, shouldn't she know the truth? Kid, if you don't get those abilities of yours under control and figure out the right people to trust—or do your own homework first—you might as well have a target on your back."

"Oh," Devi said, voice small.

Some part of me wanted to say something kind to comfort her, to relieve the look of devastation and growing fear on her face. I suppose that was natural, seeing as she'd either been set up or double-crossed…possibly both. And after all her efforts, she'd been doomed to fail today.

"You want to talk targets?" I said. "Thanks for making me one, doing whatever you did to bring all portals onto my property."

"Technically, the potential was already there. I just tweaked it," Mr. Zaki mumbled.

I ignored him, turning my glare on each of the Shades in turn. "And what do you think is going to happen when Devi's bosses find out she and Beckwell are still around? Plus, there's that mess out there in the atrium. I don't imagine you're going to clean it up, but where are all the rest of the staff? What happens to the rest of the residents if any of them get caught in the crossfire of either this battle or some other you bring here, or innocents like Mr. Whiskers get caught up in the mayhem and eaten by eagles?"

I set my lips in a mulish line and mimicked Liko standing by the door, crossing my arms over my chest. Yeah, of course I knew most of the residents could easily hold their own in a magical fight, probably better than me. But I was on a roll. It'd been a long day, I still didn't entirely understand what was going on, and damn it, I cared about the residents here and my town. But I also cared about Devi, and I felt sorry for her, and I had to keep avoiding looking at her, because then I'd feel all sorts of things all over again, and next thing I knew I'd be defending her and getting myself in even more trouble.

If you can be anything, why not be honest and kind? Dad's voice in my head gently prodded, the way he'd asked it after I came home from school after another fight, usually because the big troll kid was a big target. Or later, when I'd roll up on my bike after months away, feeling no more settled, no more satisfied with my life as a biker than I'd been here, growing up.

My gaze flicked to Devi, her head down, loose waves of dark hair hiding her expression from me, her delicate features. I'd been so concerned with not getting involved, not sure I'd remembered to be kind. If I walked away right now, left her and the Shades behind, would that be honest and kind, make me a better man than if I stayed, tried to keep the Shades and Devi out of trouble?

"I told you the cat was a bad idea," Mr. Chaimek murmured from beside Albert, leaning over his polished wood cane that was braced between his shiny loafers. "Call me George," he'd always say, especially to the ladies. A charming old rascal who'd always reminded me of some old silver-screen actor—the kind usually associated with scandal and getting some poor girl pregnant. He wore dress pants and shirts that looked like they cost more than my whole wardrobe, and he shot a warm smile to Devi, his moustache curving. "Are you feeling all right, dear?"

"Well, I just found out my new employers sent me on a mission expecting I'd explode. Not so well, actually," Devi whispered.

"The cat was fair game," Mr. Liko grouched from behind me. "We're talking saving the town, and you want me to worry about one cat?"

There was an annoyed edge to Mr. Jenklow's smile as he turned on me now. "Son, like I said on the phone, nothing would have happened to your cat." He gestured to Devi. "The lady saw to that, and if she hadn't, Teddy would have. Mr. Whiskers, I'm afraid, was simply the bait we needed to get you involved."

"Leave Mr. Whiskers alone. And I'm afraid you've got the wrong man. I don't want to be considered a fighter. The most heroic thing I do is keep all of you from busting in on Doc Quilan when it isn't your turn, and even then, sometimes you manage to sneak past me."

Mr. Jenklow just looked at me and smiled. "Heroes, Frizzly, come in all shapes, sizes, and stripes. We have a mission, and I knew exactly the man for the job."

My jaw clenched. Jenklow was off his rocker. Screw

this. Kind would be not getting involved so I didn't use my fists, so no one got hurt. "I should be going—"

Mr. Jenklow's words froze me in place. "Frizzly, do you believe Ms. Devi is dangerous and should be handled accordingly?"

I turned to Devi, who still looked like she was trying to make herself smaller and harder to see. Was she dangerous? Maybe technically, but not in her heart…or if I started thinking with other parts of my anatomy. "I, uh…I don't know if I'm the person to—"

"Ms. Devi, what do you have to say for yourself?" Jenklow said, cutting me off. "Are you a threat to Beckwell that should be dealt with accordingly? This is your chance to speak up."

"Hey, give her a minute," I said, taking a step forward, annoyance flaring through me and burning away some of my anxiety. "Who nominated you judge and jury?"

Mr. Einar leveled a look on me that made me feel like I was six years old and caught with my hand in the cookie jar. "Who else would be willing and able to do this job, Mr. Frizzly? You've just said you aren't."

"Now wait a minute, I—"

"I-I'm guilty." Devi's voice silenced us all, high-pitched and frightened.

When I turned, she'd lifted her chin and clutched her hands in front of her, twisting and twining her fingers.

She swallowed, hard, as everyone turned to stare at her, but took a deep breath and forged on. "I… I didn't want to hurt anyone—and I was assured that I wouldn't." A small frown pulled at her brow, and she dropped her gaze a moment before lifting it again. "But it would seem someone lied to me. My new employers, who likely knew as you did, sir. As Mr. Heimdall knew, as everyone who knows anything about destruction goddesses who isn't me knew." She turned to the other Shades. "No matter how small their bomb, as a destruction goddess descendant, I was likely to make it worse. Thank you, for warning me. And saving my life. I…felt things, out there, holding that bomb, a kind of power and…thirst like I've never felt before."

Hmm. Could she mean the red eyes that'd glowed the same color as the orb?

She took another shaky breath. "I could have destroyed your town. I thought I was doing it for the right reasons—not the destroying the town, of course, but setting off a small bomb that I was told would protect people who I thought were in the right. People who believe that magic and the paranormal world needs to be protected and honored. I thought I was protecting my world."

Mr. Jenklow nodded, doing a good impression of looking sympathetic. "Yes, many people who work for USELESS have been fed the same lies, especially with what little they're told."

Devi frowned, glanced back at me, then back at Mr. Jenklow and the others. "I don't work for USELESS. I mean, I did, before the restructuring plan. But I took the buyout and was happy to leave that drama behind almost a year ago."

For the first time, the old men looked disconcerted, looking from one to the other. Apparently, they hadn't expected that someone else wanted to destroy Beckwell.

It was Mr. Einar who leaned forward. "Then who do you work for?"

"The Guardians, of course."

As if they'd rehearsed it, all five of the men froze momentarily, the room becoming deathly silent as a few of them sagged back against their seats, others rubbing heads and lips.

The silence was broken when Liko swore, deeply and fluently. The biker gnomes had nothing on him.

That sick swirling feeling was back in my stomach, and I wished I was back home fertilizing my petunias.

Devi turned to me, a puzzled expression on her face. "What exactly is going on now?"

"I'm not sure… but it seems bad." I cleared my throat. "So, fellas, who are these Guardians? 'Cause I'm guessing from your reaction these schmucks aren't good."

The long silence made me edgy, and the looks exchanged by the men didn't help any.

Finally, it was Mr. Jenklow who leaned forward, resting his elbows on his bony knees. "I'd hoped we'd never have to hear that name again." He turned to Devi. "Are you certain that's what they were called? The Guardians?"

Devi frowned but nodded. "Yes, I'm quite certain. This is bad, isn't it?" She'd started twisting her fingers together and chewing on that poor abused lip of hers again.

Not that I was supposed to be thinking about her lips or her anything else. I should have been angry or at the very least wary of her. And I was? Maybe. My thoughts were all tangled up when it came to Devi, with lust, sympathy considering what she'd told me about her family, and anger and frustration that she'd dare come to my town, and try and hurt people I cared about, even if she hadn't entirely known what she was doing.

Mr. Jenklow sighed, his furry brows lowered, no trace of the usual twinkle in his blue eyes. "USELESS is bad enough; we know the kind of harm they've tried to cause and their twisted messages. But the Guardians…" He shook his head. "The Guardians worked with the German Nazis during the Second World War. Those two groups agreed on too many dangerous principles like pure races… and extermination of anyone who didn't meet their definitions of perfection. They have old, backward ideas about the paranormal races. Creatures like gods, angels, nymphs, fairies. But any creatures with even a hint of mortal blood, like werewolves, most vampires, and pretty much every soul who lives here in Beckwell… Those, they see as abominations. Attacks on their beloved purity."

That sick feeling in the pit of my stomach wasn't getting better.

"Hell, they were more extreme than the Nazis. Probably would have turned on them had they managed to win the war," Mr. Einar said, picking up for Jenklow. "They hate paranormal sanctuaries, places like Beckwell. They can't stand that we're a mix of different species and of humanity. The more extreme of their members would wipe out all of humanity given the chance."

"Thought we'd killed all those bastards during the war," Liko muttered. "Gotten rid of them the same way they destroyed those sanctuaries. Whole towns, gutted and burned, entire generations of paranormal families butchered in the streets."

"Are you sure these are the same Guardians we're talking about?" Devi said, eyes round, looking to me for the denial I couldn't give. She turned back to the group of seniors. "I never heard them say anything about mass extermination, or murder, or…or… I couldn't be part of something like that!"

"It would have been odd if they said anything so direct," Mr. Chaimek said, crossing his arms over his narrow chest, moustache and lips twisting like he'd tasted something bad. "They know most people, even their less extreme members, aren't open to murder and mayhem. At least, not to start with. So, they warm people up to the idea with talk of how paranormals have been subjugated and forced underground by the 'evil' humans. They cheer about paranormals first, strengthening our kind, that sort of rot. But when it comes down to it, they don't consider most of those who carry out their dirty work ever good enough for their 'perfect' future."

"Yes, they did talk about making us all stronger. Mother and my sister said I'd want to help with that, of course…" Devi's words dried up mid-sentence, her eyes widening as though with dawning horror.

My stomach twisted on her behalf. Gods. Her family had recruited her for these slimeball Guardians.

From her hesitation, maybe she, like me, wondered if they'd known that it was a suicide mission, too.

She turned to me again, a plea in her dark eyes, a small waver in her voice, her hands clenched at her sides but otherwise holding steady. "I'm not that kind of person. I thought… I thought I was helping our people—people that included all paranormal species. I never wanted to hurt anyone."

"Except for the part where you came here with a bomb to blow us all up," Liko growled.

Devi spun toward him. "They said it wouldn't hurt. That it would only knock out your abilities."

"I don't suppose it has time to hurt if the intensity of the explosion kills you fast enough," Mr. Zaki mused, as though doing calculations in his head. "They seemed to expect she'd explode with it, destroying us with the Senior Center. First attack. Strike before we can strike back. Classic Guardian opening gambit. Of course…if Beckwell is still standing, they're likely to try again."

Pretty sure I'd said something to that effect earlier. Not that this time it was much of a victory to be right.

"I have an old friend, a former Shade, who's insisted for years that the Guardians weren't gone. I didn't want to believe…" Mr. Jenklow rubbed a hand over his bald head.

I didn't know this former Shade. Didn't particularly care. But just standing around here while these bad guys might be planning, or worse, carrying out their next attempted attack made my stomach knot.

"What do we do about them then?" I said, speaking more loudly than I usually did and instantly getting everyone's attention.

Mr. Jenklow turned to me, a bushy white brow raised. "Are you suggesting you'd like to be part of the plan, Frizzly?"

I shifted, resettling my crossed arms. "I… No." I stole a quick glance at Devi, who still looked miserable. She needed a friend, someone to help her, someone she could trust who didn't have some other plot in mind like the Shades probably did. I couldn't seem to move my feet, couldn't seem to walk out of the room and leave her at the mercy of these dangerous old men.

"You're free to be on your way then, Frizzly," Mr. Einar said, as suspiciously agreeable as Mr. Jenklow.

"Indeed. We can deal with Ms. Devi alone. Perhaps give her some tips on survival, seeing as anyone who crosses the Guardians or tries to leave their organization without fulfilling their obligations does tend to end up dead," Mr. Chaimek added amiably.

Devi gulped, her hand going to the smooth column of her throat. "D-dead?"

"They already tried to have you blow yourself up. Is this really a surprise, kid?" Mr. Liko said, coming forward. "But nothing for you to worry about, right, Frizz?"

"Don't call me that," I said almost automatically, pulling out of Liko's reach.

Devi was blinking rapidly and had the look of someone who'd had the floor removed from beneath her…and was likely to upchuck. "I just wanted to make my family proud.

Now my bosses are going to *kill* me? I…" She looked up at me.

There was a rush of cooler air behind me as Liko opened the suite door. "Not your problem, remember? You wanted us to leave you out of this. We'll deal with Ms. Devi. Out you go," Liko said to me.

I took a step toward the door. Couldn't seem to take another one, which should have been easy. Mr. Whiskers, Edith, my petunias, my ordinary life where I didn't get involved, all of it was only a step away.

Why the hell couldn't I take that step?

Devi turned that sweet, devastated face to me, and I felt a hard pull to my insides. Ah, hell. It looked like she needed me as much or more than my suicidal cat. Which was dumb. Which was dangerous. Which might pull me into the kind of violence I feared, turn me into someone, something I couldn't respect. My head ached and I rubbed at my tight chest. Honesty and kindness. What part of that meant I could leave Devi behind?

"All right, Zaki. You must have finished your calculations and pulled the numbers by now," Jenklow said to Mr. Zaki, as though I weren't there. "What's our move?"

Skinny Mr. Zaki cocked his head, his mop of dark curls tumbling at the movement. "Well, considering that we're not yet dead, our logical counter-move would be a counter-strike. Given time, the Guardians will become as entrenched as they did before. We should prevent that at all costs, as the statistical probability of our failure and probable death only increases the more powerful they become."

"Then we go on the attack," Mr. Jenklow said, looking to the others for agreement. He glanced at me, as though surprised to find I was still there. The bugger should have gone into acting, the way he blinked at me, all wide-eyed surprise. "Is there something else, Frizzly?"

I gave him a glare. I hated admitting defeat so easily. But finally I shoved a hand back through my hair. "Maybe…" I glanced at Devi, who was looking at me with something between hope and desperation on her lovely face. Shit. I cleared my throat and focused on Jenklow instead, since there was no sense doing something any dumber than what I was already about to do. "Maybe I could, you know, help out."

I'll give Mr. Jenklow this: if he was gloating, which I'm pretty sure he was, he gave me only a polite smile instead of the self-satisfied smirk I'd expected. Instead, the old sneak turned back to the other men, asking, "Do we have any ideas then?"

Liko closed the door, then gave me a nod as he elbowed past me that was almost respectful before standing next to the sofas. "We hit back as hard and fast as they intended to hit us."

"With what?" Mr. Einar asked.

"Well," said Mr. Chaimek, a speculative gleam in his eyes as he turned his gaze on Devi. "We do happen to have a destruction goddess handy…"

Devi looked behind her, then at me. "Who? You mean… But I'm not—"

"I believe he means your grandmother," Mr. Jenklow said kindly before turning back to the others. "An attack by her would guarantee a win. If she'll help. We'll get you to her. Ideally, we'd like her to take a stand with us and Beckwell against the Guardians. In battle, she could strike a powerful blow. If she just speaks out against the Guardians, it might slow down their recruitment of other gods."

"If she's not feeling altruistic," Mr. Einar picked up, "you could point out that if the Guardians start wiping out mortals, it will mean less worshippers and less faith energy for her and other gods. They're easier to stop now, before they've re-established their power base. It wouldn't hurt if she let that kind of rumor get around to other gods, too. Again, it means the Guardians will have a hard time recruiting, and, just maybe, it will net us some allies."

Devi could only blink. "You don't think… I've never actually met her. You think I can just *ask* her to help?"

"Seems like a better idea than demanding it," Mr. Liko pointed out. "Besides, grandparents have a soft spot for grandkids, especially those named after them. You probably won't be able to return home, seeing as you didn't kill all of us. Which makes Beckwell a good place to stay, and therefore a good reason your grandmother should protect it and, by extension, you."

Devi could only blink. "I…but…"

Then she turned those big dark eyes on me, pleading silently that I do something. Be someone I wasn't. Hell, the Shades were talking about sending Devi in to meet a destruction goddess and ask for favors. It only vaguely qualified as a plan, it was away from the safety of Beckwell, and as far from "uninvolved" as you could get. All the reasons I needed to ditch this place, run home, and hide under a blanket screamed through my head.

Dad's words or some variety of them, softly spoken just like he'd say them, drowned everything else out. *If in doubt, be honest, be kind.*

I reached for Devi's hand. "It's okay. You don't have to do this alone." Somehow, I managed to resist glancing behind me at the door, at what could have been my escape. Because with Devi's warm, small fingers against mine, those other voices, other fears didn't seem so loud. "I'll go with you. I know you can do this."

She looked up at me, a tremulous smile touching her

lips. The light in her eyes and her expression made me grow a good twenty feet taller.

I eased a small breath out past my lips, tried to let the steadiness her grip offered soak through me. I believed in her, knew she could succeed. Still, no one much liked trolls, especially if they showed up unannounced—it was the whole big and scary-looking thing, I think. Well, maybe Mr. Whiskers wouldn't get his chance to turn me into garden sculpture after all. Because pretty sure asking a real destruction goddess for a favor would get me killed first.

Chapter Six

I MIGHT HAVE PROMISED Devi that I'd accompany her on the insane plan to ask her grandmother a favor. I'd meant it, too. But that didn't mean I much liked the idea, or that it hadn't made my skin as cold as stone and nausea churn in my belly. I trusted Devi. Still wasn't sure about the Shades. Sacrificial goat wasn't exactly a role I wanted to play.

But the rest of the Shades were getting up from the sofas, talking ingredients, timelines, and calculations, leaving Devi and me standing there. Maybe someone planned on getting a bell for around my neck. Gods.

So why aren't you just leaving? my inner voice mocked me.

I rolled my shoulders, not that it made them ache less. Sure, could have chalked up my bad decision-making to a pretty face and loneliness, and Devi was definitely a big part of why I'd agreed to go. I also had no death wish, being turned to stone or otherwise. But I couldn't seem to stop thinking how I'd feel if I went home now, left Devi and the Shades behind, only to find out later something had gone wrong. I'd always wonder, have those regrets. All of which seemed likelier to turn me into someone I didn't want to face in the mirror just as fast or faster than using my fists.

"They want me to go talk to Bibiji? The *real* Devi?" Devi said, leaning closer to me, the soft perfume scent of her—something almost floral, a bit spicy wafting over me.

I frowned a little. "You know, I get that you're not her, but that doesn't make you any less real. Does it?"

She blinked at me a second, as though the idea had never occurred to her. "I… suppose so. It's just, that's how my family always refers to her, to both of us really. She's the Real Devi the Destroyer, and I'm…" Her shoulders fell, along with her gaze. "My sister and my mother convinced me I should work for the Guardians. They're descended from Devi, too. If they knew what might happen to me…"

Then they were scum, sending her into that situation. But she'd figure that out for herself. The life I'd lived, I wasn't up to casting stones.

Still, I reached out a hand and touched the soft back of her elbow, trying to ignore the crazy firework sensation that ripped through me. "Maybe they had no idea. And in the end, you didn't do it." I offered her a crooked smile. "You sure did show that eagle, though."

Her smile brightened the entire room, the grumbles and chatter from the old men fading. "Maybe." She looked down a little for a moment, then back, color climbing her face. "You must think I'm such a fool for joining the Guardians, believing the things I did, like about the babies and the internet."

I couldn't help but lean just a little closer, get a little nearer to her warmth, her soft scent, the brush of her unbound hair against my forearm. "I've fallen in with the wrong people and made bad decisions, too. Dad said it was just part of figuring out who you are—maybe by figuring out who you're not."

She considered me a moment or two longer, long enough I was tempted to squirm.

"You've always been so honest with me. Even when you suspected I might be dangerous. Which is why I want…" She swallowed, hands twisting together before she seemed to force herself to meet my eyes before she continued. "I want you to know, what happened back at your house—not with Mr. Whiskers, but with, uh, the salve, and us…and the touching—"

I cleared my throat, leaning in closer, catching more of her scent, my reaction to her as strong as it'd ever been. "You don't have to—"

"It wasn't an act," she said, cutting me off from telling her she didn't have to make excuses.

Now it was me staring, searching her expression for a hint of the lie, her angle, some reason she'd tell me this now. Because she wanted me to come with her? Because she was afraid of going alone? Maybe because she wanted someone to speak up for her if the Shades turned on her.

Yet, she smiled at me. Her gaze was open and vulnerable, face darkening in color as she reached for my hand. "I, uh…" She dropped her gaze a moment before peeking back up at me through her lashes. "I'm sorry I wasn't completely honest with you earlier. But for what it's worth, I'm glad these men decided to bring us together. I'm glad I met you. You're the sweetest, most beautiful man—and troll—I've ever met, inside and out."

I could only gape. My brain stuttered again. Some part of me, a cynical part, tried to whine that this had to be an angle, but I ignored that voice. Didn't make much sense for it to be an angle, not when I'd already agreed to accompany her. I swallowed, hard, a kind of weightlessness suffusing me, probably putting a goofy-ass smile on my face. Damned if I cared.

Because if what Devi said wasn't a ploy, wasn't an angle… then maybe she liked me for just me. Same way I liked her.

"Ms. Devi, Heimdall mentioned another of your talents lay in portals and reality bubbles. I was wondering if you might be able to assist us with some of the calculations and the location," Mr. Jenklow said, interrupting us and sadly reminding me not only were we still reluctant participants in a dangerous plan that was likely to get us killed sooner rather than later.

We turned together to face him.

Devi's fingers brushed close to mine, sending fireworks and something more…something tremulous, perhaps even more dangerous than trying to reason with a destruction goddess on her turf.

Hope.

Devi's dark eyes widened, and her voice rose in pitch. "You want *my* help? But… I worked for the Guardians." She dropped her gaze. "And if you asked anyone for a reference, they'd say I was more likely to fail my mission than complete it. Look what happened here."

Mr. Jenklow stepped closer, put a gentle hand on her shoulder. "Ms. Devi, defying those orders and choosing to *not* harm people was an act of courage and strength. You should be proud. You are a singular being, even in your own family."

She seemed like she wanted to deny what the old man was telling her and looked to the other four old men who'd gathered around, then back at me.

What she appeared to find in our expressions made her take a deep breath, straighten her shoulders, stand a little taller. "I… I could probably find her," she said, a hint of something like confidence in her voice. "She uses a private reality bubble. And, well—" she shrugged, "—I've always been rather good at making those. Mother and Father said—"

"Probably nothing good," I couldn't help but mutter.

She looked at me, a dark eyebrow arching upward.

"You can form your own reality bubble?" Mr. Zaki said, voice awed and turning her attention away from me. "I've always understood only especially powerful beings are capable of such."

Devi blinked. Then leaned forward, whispering in a voice that seemed almost afraid to dare be heard. "Really? I thought… It's rather like painting to me. I just thought it was an unusual hobby no one was interested in. My family certainly wasn't."

Mr. Jenklow and the others just smiled before they gathered around Devi and began to chat animatedly about reality bubbles, how to make them, how to find them, and how they'd essentially "break into" the one that belonged to her grandmother.

I crossed my arms and narrowed my eyes. Now wasn't that convenient, that she was able to do exactly what they needed her to be able to do, a rare ability to create and access reality bubbles. After the Shades had heard from Heimdall, it seemed like maybe they'd started planning what would happen if Devi showed up. They might have been surprised that the Guardians were involved, but they seemed more than happy to forge alliances with destruction goddesses no matter the enemy.

Mr. Einar broke away from the group clustered around Devi and came back to stand beside me. "So, are you ready to accompany her, Frizzly?"

I turned to him. Pretty sure I was the goat in this plan,

at least according to the Shades. "Why don't you go, Mr. Einar? You can talk anyone into doing anything."

He paused, raising a brow. "You talked Sister Marguerite into leaving her clothes *on* for her doctor's appointment. There are some miracles even I can't manage. Perhaps you underestimate yourself."

I shrugged. That was just part of my job, talking people into doing things they didn't really want to do. Come to think of it, I'd done a little of that even when I'd started in maintenance, talking people into not walking on the lawn or incinerating all the flowers by dumping failed potions out their windows. Most people weren't in the doctor's office because it gave them the warm fuzzies, but because they had to be. I just tried to make it easier—on them and Doc Quilan.

I turned to look at Devi, working with the four other old men, explaining things, looking excited and… happy. Apparently, they were onto the step of the plan where they somehow got Devi and I to the destruction goddess' home. Sure, Heimdall had passed on tips about the potential he saw in Devi, but the Shades seemed to appreciate and recognize those skills in a way even her own family hadn't.

I adjusted my crossed arms, palms damp and my brow furrowed. If they'd seen that potential in Devi, was there more reason they'd involved me in their plans to protect Beckwell other than my affinity for stone?

Still, when barely an hour later, I stood next to Devi in front of a whirling silver portal that looked like certain death, I wasn't sure I wanted anyone to see more in me. Petrification by cat was starting to look like a charming way to go. My brain and self-preservation instinct screamed that I should run, that any participation in this harebrained scheme was going to get me killed because that's what doing hero shit usually did to people. Or in my case, people around me usually got hurt. I turned to Devi. No way could I let that happen this time. I squeezed my hand into a fist.

"So, uh, this leads to your grandma, huh?" I said to Devi, who stood beside me, her face gray. My gaze returned, helplessly, to the portal's swirling silver-death.

"Yes," she said quietly. "Knowing where a reality bubble is, like the one Bibiji lives in, well, it's kind of like a moving address." She shrugged. "Mr. Zaki did most of the calculations. I've always been more intuitive than precise about locating them, but same thing, I suppose. I've never entered one uninvited, though."

I mean, I understood reality bubbles in a vague sense, had learned about them in school. Truly powerful beings could create a bubble within reality and form their own mini world. Within that mini world, physics and reality were warped to the creator's preference, the very existence of the thing invisible without permission or equally powerful magic to find it.

Which made Devi more powerful than she thought, if she used to create these things as a kid.

It also meant that basically, we were breaking and entering into a destruction goddess' personal bubble. If the whirling silver portal didn't kill us, stood to reason she would. No one liked being surprised by a troll.

"Remember: we can't keep this portal open for too long. Someone would notice the energy surge, Loki or one of the Four if our luck is especially bad," Mr. Jenklow explained again, like he'd done while Chaimek and Devi did whatever they'd needed to do to open the whirly gateway in the first place.

After the day it'd been, I really didn't want to have to deal with Loki, too.

"Do what you can to convince her to help us, ideally

speaking out against the Guardians and speaking up for Beckwell. If she agrees to help us stop the Guardians now, we could save thousands of lives," Mr. Einar said, picking up from Jenklow seamlessly.

I'd noticed they did that a lot, like they'd had a lot of time to learn to finish each other's sentences.

"Be sure to stay with Devi, Frizzly. You're our lodestone, the way we can find you. You carry Beckwell and all its hopes with you," Mr. Chaimek said.

I gulped. No pressure or anything.

"Of course, if someone finds us before you get back and the gate is shut, even if the goddess doesn't kill you first, you're screwed buddy," Liko said with an almost-smile.

They could all kind of finish each other's sentences. Like an experienced team who'd worked together a lot longer than any of us had known their little group existed. Still wasn't sure whether the idea made me feel better…or more nervous.

Mr. Einar put a hand on my shoulder.

I flinched in spite of myself, turning back toward the portal.

"Just be yourself, Frizzly, and you'll do fine," Henry said smoothly. "We're counting on it."

Well, that seemed like a really bad idea. I was a half-troll. No one counted on a troll. *I* wouldn't count on a troll. There were probably dozens of people in Beckwell more qualified for this than me. To be both brains and brawn. To remember to still be kind and honest when my back was against the wall.

"I-I've always wanted to meet Bibiji. But the stories I've heard…" Devi turned to me, her face ashen, eyes large and dark. She looked as terrified as I felt. "Are you sure you want to come with me?" She gulped, facing the silver whirlpool. "I have to go. I have to try and make up for the mistakes I've made. You could go home. Pet Mr. Whiskers for me. Perhaps forgive me when you see your food preparation room."

She'd been dumped here in Beckwell, expected to do something her jackass bosses knew she'd fail at. Hell, it'd been a suicide mission, and she'd been desperate for it because somehow, all the idiots she'd been surrounded with for most of her life didn't seem to be able to see the amazing woman she was. Smart, kind, inventive, brave. All that and more, so far out of my league we weren't even playing the same sport.

But she'd saved me and Mr. Whiskers even when everyone had expected her to do something different. I wouldn't, *couldn't* abandon her now. All we had to do was show her grandmother how amazing Devi was, and if the real Devi the Destroyer was as powerful and smart as the Shades seemed to think, then all I had to do was show her what I saw. We'd get our favor, get the goddess to agree to stand up against the Guardians with us, and everything would be sunshine.

Certainty settled the tenseness in my shoulders and the queasiness in my belly, and I gave her a smile I hoped gave off the impression of confidence and not nausea. "Yeah. I'm sure."

I held out my hand to her.

Her lips curved in a tremulous smile as she reached her fingers toward mine. At the bare touch, those fireworks went off right on cue. Damn, but I could get used to that…and sure would like to someday see what other kind of fireworks we could make together.

I never took my eyes off hers as I stepped into the whirlpool first, Devi right at my side.

Mostly, the whirlpool or portal felt cold against my

skin, the way it did when I transformed into stone. Except the part where it was trying to turn me to stone inside out, while ripping me to pieces and sending all those parts to other sides of the universe, while also simultaneously sticking me back together. I grit my teeth and focused on Devi's fingers in mine…and the fact that somewhere, I had fingers. We whirled and were tossed, backward, inside-out, sideways. Again and again.

And then it was over.

We stepped out into a cobblestone courtyard surrounded by tall pink archways and a regal, multi-storied building of the same pink stone. Water burbled in a nearby fountain with small, raised waterways running off it in both directions. The warm air was scented with flowers and brushed against my skin as softly as a lover's kiss. Potted palms stood sentinel around the courtyard and swayed in the soft breeze. An exotic retreat, it was how I'd imagined the courtyards of the ancient sultans, sun gently warming my back…

Hold on… Sun *warming* my back? Not turning me to stone?

Cautiously, I held out a hand, the subtle warmth of the light tickling over my skin. I sucked in a breath at the sensation.

Devi looked to me, her smile tremulous.

It struck me how she was possibly more beautiful, bathed in the late-day sun that kissed her cheeks and created a red halo around her hair. Despite all my reservations, it seemed that for once in my life, I was exactly where I wanted *and* was supposed to be.

"How dare you invade my domain?" a furious female voice roared from behind Devi and me.

We exchanged a wide-eyed look before we spun. I raised my hands more out of habit than anything else. I was a big guy. Whatever I could do to look less dangerous, the better. No troll surprises, remember?

A woman with skin slightly darker than Devi's stood behind us, her hands on her hips, wearing a majestic blue sari with gold embroidery, her long, black, silver-streaked hair pulled back in a braid. She glared at us, murder glittering in her dark eyes. "Well? Who are you? You have three seconds to convince me not to kill you. Lucky for you I'm wearing my favorite sari today. I don't need it ruined with splatter."

My throat squeezed. I wished my imagination didn't supply what kind of splatter she meant.

Fortunately, Devi was quicker that I was, reaching for my hand, tugging it down and squeezing it in hers as she took a small step forward. "Bibiji—grandmother—we mean no disrespect. I'm Parmeet and Neil's daughter, your namesake actually…or does that make you mine? I'm not sure if Mother and Father mentioned me, and we've been, um, busy. Sorry I didn't visit earlier."

Nice, save for the reality that her parents were dicks who couldn't see how great their daughter was, and therefore hadn't bothered to introduce her.

"This is my…" Devi's words stumbled and she shot me a quick look, color staining her cheekbones, making her even prettier.

Yeah, not the best time to be noticing these things, but then again, there was a chance I'd only have these last few seconds left of life, and admiring Devi wasn't the worst thing to do with the time.

"This is Frizzly," Devi finished quickly. "We're here to beg your favor."

The older woman's eyes narrowed on me, and she crossed her arms. "What kind of name is Frizzly?" she demanded of me.

"A strange one. A leprechaun lied to my father and told him it was a troll name," I said quickly.

Devi squeezed my fingers in encouragement.

"A troll," the goddess said with a sneer.

"Half-troll. Ma'am," I said, talking quickly. What were you supposed to call a goddess anyway?

"He's a good man," Devi added quickly. "He risked his life to save his cat, and then to speak on my behalf and try to help me. He accompanied me here, knowing it would be dangerous. Please, Bibiji, will you hear what I have to say?"

Disapproval bracketed her lips, and she tapped a foot. "You invaded my home and now have the gall to demand anything of me?"

"Our most sincere apologies," I said. "Obviously, you have more worthwhile things to occupy you, so we ask for only a short audience. Or rather, your granddaughter does. She has shown tremendous courage and ability already in her aid of me and others today, never mind the poise that she certainly inherited from you. I understand if you wish to speak with her alone. Another visitor so interesting is unlikely to visit any time soon."

The goddess considered me a long moment or two before she finally rolled her darkly kohled eyes, then flung up her hands and turned, a graceful move. She headed for the arches leading into the temple. "This sounds like it will take a while. I need tea anyway."

Devi and I glanced at each other. Just Devi? The two of us?

She stopped, glanced at us over her shoulder. "Well? Come on then. Both of you. The troll can stay…so long as he's house-trained."

I bit the inside of my lip, but considering I wasn't suicidal, this definitely wasn't the time to correct troll prejudice. I followed Devi and her grandmother through the courtyard and through one of the silk-curtained entrances.

The inside of the temple was as sumptuous as the courtyard. Seriously. Sumptuous wasn't a word I threw around every day, but with the jewel-toned carpets layering the floor, silken pillows and furnishings for lounging, and yet another trickling water-fountain inside, this had to be the most luxurious home I'd ever entered. I tried not to stare, especially considering the goddess' reaction to any hint of troll; I didn't need to prove her prejudices right.

She lounged back on a turquoise and gold chaise, curling her bare feet up and under the folds of her sari.

Devi and I perched on the edge of the sofa-like thing across from her, and I clasped my knees to check if they were shaking.

The goddess snapped her fingers, and a graceful, curving glass table appeared between us and her, loaded with an ornate tea service with cups for three and snacks stacked high on a tiered display. She poured herself some tea, then into the two opposite cups for us, took some of the treats before once more settling back against the chaise.

"Take your tea, drink, and tell me your sob story then," she said, no warmth in her voice. She shot me another glare over the edge of her teacup.

Obediently, Devi and I reached for our teacups. I drank mine down faster than I probably should have, wishing it was something a hell of a lot stronger.

Devi cradled her teacup in her lap and launched into the story of how we'd ended up here, beginning with how she'd taken a job with the Guardians to prove herself to her family—and the goddess. She brushed over some of the trouble she had with destruction and controlling her abilities, moving into her mission to destroy Beckwell, how she'd met me, how dangerous the Guardians were to all paranormal beings, and how she was under threat from Beckwell and the Guardians with no solution in sight unless the goddess could somehow intervene.

Throughout the explanation, the goddess had sipped at her tea, both hands curled around the cup as she considered us both over the edge of the rim. The only sound in the room was the trickling fountain and the screech of what I was pretty sure were peacocks from somewhere outside.

Of course, I could barely hear anything beyond the pounding of my own heart, and my hands were probably going to leave damp spots on the knees of my jeans.

"We'd like you to help defend the paranormal sanctuary of Beckwell from the Guardians, who want—"

"I care nothing for paranormal sanctuaries, including Beckwell," the goddess interrupted.

Devi swallowed and tried again. "But Beckwell is special. It's a collection of so many species, so many good people—"

"Pass. Not my problem," the goddess said, waving a hand and looking disinterested.

I cautiously cleared my throat, and her gaze sliced toward me. "Respectfully, if the Guardians take over Beckwell, that's just the beginning. They'll eventually destroy all mortals, many of whom may be your worshippers. No mortals means no worshippers, no faith energy. If you help us stop the Guardians now, it preserves your power. I might be wrong, but that definitely sounds like your business."

The look she gave me could have incinerated, but fortunately, she turned away with a sniff before there was any permanent damage, sipping at her tea.

"Well? Will you help us? Will you speak out against the Guardians and defend Beckwell?" Devi asked softly, with more daring than I had, a small tremble in her words.

I'd played my hand and knew better than to open my mouth again.

Devi offered the goddess a sickly smile, lifting a shaking teacup to her lips.

The goddess' lips tightened, and she leaned forward to set her teacup on the small table. "You are young and lack patience, child."

"And discipline, possibly direction. Definitely missing some social niceties, at least according to Mother and Father. That's part of why they never wanted to introduce me," Devi said, then flushed, ducking her eyes. "I'm sorry. I don't know why I told you that."

"Because what you lack in the charms usually associated with a dutiful daughter, you make up for in ambition, personal strength, and honesty." The goddess' voice softened. "Those are not things for which you should apologize, child."

Devi looked up, blinking.

The knot in my stomach loosened, just a bit. Maybe we would get out of this alive *and* with the help we needed.

The goddess shrugged, and something in her expression gentled. "Did you know, in all my very long existence, with all my children and descendants, that you are the first to truly try and make something of yourself rather than just live off my generosity and the strength of my believers? The rest of my family? Useless twits. But you, child, *you* have potential. Not as a true destruction goddess of course. But our family already has one of those. You shall be something else. You too shall be remembered, shall be worthy, if not in quite as many hearts as I."

Devi cleared her throat and blinked rapidly, her eyes shining and bright. "Y-you think I…that I might be worth something?" She'd reacted similarly when Jenklow had praised her abilities, making me think this was maybe the first time anyone had truly recognized her potential.

Also made me want to put a fist through something, because damn. Was everyone else blind?

The slightest of smiles curved the goddess' face, and I could see that, once, she had been as beautiful as Devi, or perhaps even more so. "You bear my name, a token of greatness. It is fate that you achieve greatness, and whatever you choose to do with it, you will prove yourself worthy."

Seeing that she was smiling and less worried about getting splatter on her sari, I dared to quietly interject. "So…does this mean you'll help us protect Beckwell? That you'll speak out against the Guardians, stand against them and prevent them from rising?"

Her expression hardened as it turned on me. "I care nothing for you, nor for a town of mortals who are not my worshippers. None of my worshipers are in your Beckwell, so if it's lost, it costs me nothing. Should the Guardians come for my worshippers, then and only then will I ensure they regret it. I will make clear my fondness for my granddaughter—and my displeasure should anything untoward happen to her. But these Guardians and the affairs of the mortal world remain up to the Fates and mortals. If mortals are worth saving, they'll figure out how to save themselves." She unfolded herself from the chaise.

"But, Bibiji, please, respectfully, if you could just help the town this once—" Devi began.

The goddess set her teacup down with a hard clink and stood.

Devi and I quickly set our teacups back on the table that vanished as soon as they touched it. We scrambled to our feet.

"No. I told you. I care nothing for a town of mortals

who care nothing for me." The goddess again sent a softer expression in Devi's direction. "But I will be watching you, my granddaughter, eager to see where your path takes you next. You will have tea with me again." Again, no such warmth as she turned to me. "You will never come here again without invitation, or I will have a new sculpture for my garden." She gave me a terrifying, slightly lewd smile. "I prefer nudes."

I was still deciding how to react when the goddess flicked her hand, like shooing a fly.

My skin and bones seemed to dissolve before they whirled around like water rushing through a waterslide—up, then down, then backward, then sideways. Gods, I hated this part.

Chapter Seven

I'D HAVE BEEN sick if I'd had a stomach in that swirling void as the whirling feeling intensified, but my entire essence had been blended to goo. It only got worse as my bones, muscles, and skin solidified just in time to slam me into the gray industrial carpet in Mr. Jenklow's suite, back in Beckwell. Apparently being immune to most magic didn't make the whole transportation through magical portals any less crappy. To think that this could have been an ordinary Tuesday, dealing with paperwork and patients. No angry destruction goddesses, no scary groups trying to destroy my town, no getting tossed through magical portals.

No Devi. My shoulders tightened at the idea.

A warm shadow, scented of Devi, was near me, and her soft fingers caressed my face. "Frizzly? Are you okay?"

I tried to assure her I was, since that was the right thing to do, but my tongue wasn't working properly yet and I managed only some unintelligible mumbles. Well, at least Devi seemed to have recovered faster. Maybe my troll side had made magical transportation worse.

I lay there a moment, taking stock of my body parts, checking if they were in the right places. All good…even if our situation was now worse. We'd failed, at least when it came to protecting Beckwell or stopping these Guardian guys before things got worse. That's what you got for sending someone like me to save the town rather than someone more qualified.

The old men scrambled around, peppering us with questions, but the words all jumbled together as if my ears hadn't quite connected to my brain, or maybe because I didn't give a crap yet. The men remained blurry blobs of various shades and colors around me, and that one guy poking me with the tip of his cane.

I reluctantly opened my eyes and lifted my head enough to turn and find Devi hovering over me. The smear of red and light brown cleared to become her beautiful soft smile, the concern in her dark eyes, delicate tendrils of dark hair framing her tear-stained face. It took all my focus and strength to force my arm into movement, to move it the few inches necessary until my fingers touched hers, to reassure myself she was real, she was here, and she was safe.

She knelt beside me, but other than a faint gray tinge to her skin, when she reached for my hand, she seemed relatively unharmed. "I was so afraid…" She gulped. "I'm glad you're okay. At least I didn't mess that up and get you hurt."

Hurt and okay were relative terms. But I was conscious enough to feel those sparks dance between us at just the light contact of our hands, and I managed to squeeze her tiny fingers in mine. It was almost like her touch returned some small amount of my strength.

Then her hand was gone, and the world dipped and whirled. My stomach flipped, and my knees were as soft as mushy peas. Aw, damn. Seemed like they were trying to get me off the floor. I squeezed my lips closed against the rising nausea as Mr. Einar tugged and pulled at me, at least trying to be gentle. On my other side was the bigger Mr. Liko, who'd never heard of the word gentle.

I tried to focus on Devi, who rose lithely to her feet, watching me with concern. My stomach lurched again. I couldn't have made it to the sofa without Einar and Liko half-carrying me, and I settled heavily onto the groaning furniture. It hadn't been my day, and to make matters worse, I kept making an ass of myself in front of Devi. Dad's reminder that there was more to me than just my strength wasn't helping. I'd still gotten involved, got a headache for my trouble and didn't help anyone.

I rubbed my forehead. Everything hurt, and the Shades were asking a lot of questions again. They were less blurry, solidifying back into grumpy, trouble-making old men who seemed determined to make my life more difficult.

One of the questions finally seemed to get through to my brain. "So? Is she going to help us?" Mr. Jenklow asked.

"She basically said she'd put in a good word for me, but no, she won't help with the Guardians, won't help defend Beckwell," Devi said softly with a sigh. "Maybe if I try to reason with the Guardians—"

Liko barked with laughter. "Yeah, that'll go over well." He blew out a breath. "Well, guess that's it then. We're screwed."

"Don't be so melodramatic," Mr. Chaimek snapped at Liko.

"It's called reality. Sugar-coating it won't make it better," Liko said, getting in the other man's face. "We've lost almost two days already."

I was on my feet between them, swaying slightly, before

I'd ever officially decided to intervene. "Look. Why don't we all just take a step back, and maybe a few breaths, huh? And what do you mean we've lost two days?"

Now Liko was in my face. "Well, genius, time moves differently in a reality bubble. You and Ms. Trouble have been gone almost two days. You had a mission. You failed. Now we're out of time because the Four and Loki are back in town, and all varieties of shit are about to rain down." His lips twisted in a sneer. "Why they ever wanted to recruit you, I sure the hell can't see."

I refused to back down, Liko and I practically nose to nose. Recruit me? For what? I'd made it clear from the beginning that I wasn't in the hero business, and whatever their schemes, I didn't want a part of them. I mean, look how well things had gone with the destruction goddess and getting her help. I barely understood who or what the Guardians were—other than they were bad.

"Liko!" Jenklow said sharply.

Liko growled and spun away.

"Frizzly, let us explain—"

"No, that's fine," I said, my voice sharp. I'd heard enough at this point. I mean, it'd been a hell of a day, and it was still hard to stand, let alone argue with these old fools.

I gave them all a tight smile but had to avoid Devi's gaze and the disappointment I knew I'd find there. What had I expected? That somehow we'd have some kind of happy ending? I was a troll. She was a demi-goddess. We were literally from two different worlds, and it was about damned time we both remembered that.

I met Mr. Jenklow and Mr. Einar's gazes evenly since they seemed to be the ones in charge. "I'm glad the Four are back because it means the right people for the job will finally be here to protect the town. Tell them what's going on. And next time, whatever your scheme is, leave me and Mr. Whiskers the hell out of it." I turned and walked to the door, more strength returning to my legs the more I moved.

I made it out the door and into the hall, now more active with the usual level of residents moving around and chatting with each other. The small hand that caught my elbow brought me to a stop.

I closed my eyes with a sigh. "Devi, I'm sorry. I…" What the hell was I supposed to say that I hadn't been saying all day? This wasn't my gig. I wasn't some guru when it came to talking people into anything. Look at how it'd gone with her grandmother. I was better off sticking to what I knew: my cat, my bike, my petunias, and my job. That's it, that's all. "I can't do this," I found myself saying.

"I know."

My shoulders slumped.

"Frizzly, can you… Will you look at me? Please?" Devi asked.

The other residents gathered around us, forming an audience in case something interesting happened. It was one of their favorite forms of entertainment, but I wasn't up to playing dancing monkey today.

I tried to ignore them as I turned to Devi reluctantly.

Her eyes shone with moisture, but she offered me a small smile. "Some day, huh?"

I shrugged.

She bit her lip a moment, a small frown tugging at her brows. "I…" She swallowed, then straightened again. "Thank you for coming with me to see Bibiji. For everything you've done today. I've contributed to this mess, but maybe, before I go home—I mean, if I survive and all—maybe I could, uh…" She dropped her gaze and her shoulders drooped. “Maybe I’ll stop by. To visit Mr. Whiskers.”

Mr. Whiskers. Right. It was a bit hard to breathe, and the pain blooming in my chest was probably just a side-effect of the portal travel. No damned way was I allowing it to be anything else. “Yeah. Sure. If you like. He’d like that.” I wanted to turn and walk away, but I couldn’t seem to convince my feet to move. “Devi, I… Good luck, okay? Be careful, and don’t trust everything those old guys tell you. Or what anyone tells you, for that matter. You make your own decisions about the truth. And in case anyone tells you different, you’re an intelligent, powerful, beautiful woman. I hope you don’t forget that.”

Finally, my feet seemed satisfied with my complete humiliation, I gave her a nod, and then turned and walked away. This time, her hand didn’t stop me. Not when I reached the end of the hall and the central atrium, somehow miraculously restored to its usual general order. Although the faint scent of charred rubber and a few new burn marks on the parts of the sofas not covered with residents hinted it wasn’t entirely set aright.

One of the nurses was at the station again, but the lights were off in the med clinic. For a second, I wondered if the doc had taken a vacation, but two days lost meant now it was early Thursday, when the doc did his out of clinic rounds. Forgetting to take vacation days was something we usually had in common. Maybe I should have investigated, but instead I let my feet carry me out through the double-glass sliding doors instead. I couldn’t remember the last time I’d taken a sick day, and it was a good day to take one.

I needed to go home, dig in my garden, pet Mr. Whiskers, and try to forget today, the stupid ideas I’d had, and the idiotic hope for anything different.

Edith waited outside for me without judgment, and I clipped the helmet onto the seat behind me before I straddled the bike, trying to ignore the image of Devi's delighted smile when we'd arrived at the Center, her joy over her first motorcycle ride. I started the bike, backed out of the stall, and turned around to head back out on the road. Maybe I'd take the long way home, try to clear my head.

Devi would be fine. She was powerful, and she had a goddess looking out for her. Edith and I crunched out through the gravel parking lot, past the community hall and the library. Mr. Jenklow, despite his scheming, wouldn't intentionally let anything happen to Devi or put her in danger. I was fairly sure of that.

I reached the corner leading onto the road and to the four-way stop. Frowned at the crowd of vehicles clogging it, and an uneasy itch started at the nape of my neck. RVs, cars, vans…there was the new police chief's truck near the edge of it. And that might be the black pseudo ice-cream truck that belonged to Famine over there, too. I scowled at the traffic, at the dull din of people all trying to talk at once that seemed to be happening on the other side of all those vehicles.

I glanced the other way down the road, toward open highway, almost as empty as usual. I could open Edith up out there, just enjoy the wind and the bike and the day. I could make that a really long route back home. I'd said to myself how many times today that I wasn't the tights and cape kind of guy. I didn't need to get involved. I'd made enough mistakes already for several lifetimes. A quiet, unassuming life was all I wanted. All I needed.

The voices from the crowd were getting louder. More impatient. More afraid.

Well, hell.

I closed my eyes a second, grimaced. Whatever else was true, whatever else happened, this was still my town, these were still my people. The cape might not fit, but I couldn't just go home and hide when my town needed help. I turned back toward the four-way, and Edith and I headed into the fray.

Chapter Eight

I PARKED Edith near the blue metal Emergency Response building, just outside of the crowd and the four-way stop, before I strode into the thick mass of people, winding my way through the assorted vehicles and strangers. The advantage of being a big guy was that when people saw me coming, they generally moved out of the way. I still didn't know what the hell was going on, other than this group of people didn't seem to be regular Beckwell citizens, and that the center of the action was near the black Famine ice cream truck. That was my destination then. I'd figure out the details as I went.

Of course, when I got close enough to see around the vehicles and the crowd of people, some of whom had children on their shoulders, my insides twisted to see Loki—another big guy. My day had already been pretty shitty without getting tangled in whatever he was up to... Making things worse, the Four were also there. To look at them, they just looked like four attractive women I'd gone to school with. Nothing about their looks, from the petite, dark-haired Death to the tall, curvy, red-headed Famine to the pale and blonde Pestilence or even the dark-haired War with her long braid hinted at how powerful they were. Backing them up were their husbands. War had married Loki. There was the blond guy I didn't know well who'd married Famine. Then the two big Quilan twins had married Death and Pestilence respectively, both brothers powerful in town as the new police chief and the town doctor—my boss.

I hesitated, getting jostled by the crowd that grew more agitated, pressing closer to the Four. All day I'd been hoping someone more qualified for dealing with big paranormal problems would step in and save the day. These people in front of me? They *were* those people. Who did I think I was, getting involved?

War, though, jerked on her brown braid seemingly in irritation, keeping her lips firmly sealed, clutching her husband, Loki's, hand and glaring at the crowd. Frankly, none of us needed her talking right now, since the power of her voice would just rile everyone up more.

Loki wasn't even paying attention to the crowd, his tight jaw and expression fixed on the two strangers beside them. One of them a tall man with deep-green skin and horns, perhaps a demon. The other had pale skin, a haughty expression, and wore white robes. Only a god would be arrogant enough to pull that look off.

Which left the other three horsewomen to face the crowd. And they weren't doing so well.

Death, petite and dark haired, shouted at the crowd. "We don't have time for this right now. Please, go home," she cried, waving her arms at them, which only seemed to make the crowd shout louder.

"I could give you cupcakes. Would cupcakes help?" Red-haired and curvy Famine tried next.

"This isn't working," pale-haired Pestilence said, looking worriedly back at her husband and friends.

"Come on, everyone. Time to clear the intersection," Chief Quilan said. A tall, bronzed skin man in uniform, his presence alone usually helped settled the peace.

The crowd swarmed toward the Four.

Pestilence let out a little yelp.

They really sucked at this. The crowd control, organizing people. Maybe honest and kind didn't have to mean being uninvolved. Just like maybe helping others didn't have to mean violence. I took a deep breath then forged forward through the crowd, politely trying to shove my way to the front. Again, big meant the sea of people parted for me.

Doc Quilan looked up when he spotted me, relief filling his expression. He offered me a hand, pulling me toward them. "Frizzly. Boy, am I glad to see you."

"What's going on?" I said, raising my voice to be heard above the crowd.

The doctor looked almost baffled. "They just…all showed up. From every direction, all arriving here. They said they saw us on the internet or something? Now they're demanding that we do something to help them, but it's not like we have hotels or suitable accommodations, especially not for this many people."

"Hey, big guy," Death said to me. Shorter than even Devi, but with similar brown skin, her head barely reached mid-chest on me. "Want to wave your arms around a lot and holler to scare these idiots off? I do not have time for this. You have no idea the headaches my reapers and I have been dealing with since the fall of the Veils. The dead have nowhere to go, nothing to do but, apparently, irritate me and keep the kids awake."

"I don't think scaring these people is going to help," I

said mildly, keeping it polite on the basis that Death scared me.

"Then what do we say? What do we tell them?" Famine said, wringing her hands and shooting nervous smiles at the angry crowd, which meant now none of the Four were even trying to talk to the crowd. There were dark circles under the pretty Famine's green eyes, and she stood almost as tall as some of the men.

"Oh, Frizzly. You've got to help us!" Pestilence said, grabbing my upper arm. My boss' wife, we were almost friends…except that I was always uncomfortably aware she was my boss' wife.

I stood stiffly until she pulled away. This wasn't how this was supposed to play out. These were the heroes. This was their schtick. So why were they doing such a crappy job with it?

"Stop smothering him, Piper," War finally said impatiently, tugging Pestilence away from me and giving me an icy blue glare that made me wish I was dealing with Loki instead. She considered the crowd, considered the men, the god and the demon, then me, lips tightly pressed together before she grabbed my collar and leaned forward. "We don't have time for this shit," she said, voice pitched low for me. "Those nimrods over there—" She nodded at the people Loki was dealing with.

Loki had his arms crossed over his chest, his eyebrow raised and his stare glassy while the god and demon flailed their hands and shouted at each other.

War continued. "They're insisting they're the de facto leaders of Beckwell because they were the mayors or some such in the Braelyn and Daimoleigh versions of Beckwell." She gestured toward another group.

Some of this group I recognized as locals, most of them jostling with others beside them.

"Those people are in fights over land claims because other people and castles showed up on their land when the Veils came down, most of the new arrivals demons." Then War shook her head at the rest of the crowd. "And them, they somehow think we can save them or something. Damned internet. Some of them are here because they have newly emerged abilities, some of them need sanctuary, some of them are just bloody tourists." She leaned forward. "I am a librarian. This is not in the job description. What do we do about them? How do we deal with them?"

If Death scared me, War freaking terrified and awed me. Had even when we'd gone to school together, before she'd come into her full powers. Come to think of it, it was just who she was.

Since the Veils had come down—thanks to the Four—they'd become the accepted leaders not only for Beckwell, a rapidly swelling boomtown of paranormal activity. But they were also expected, because of their immense power and how dithering the gods always were, to be diplomats of the paranormal world out into the world of the Normals, who were now confronted with and terrified by the reality of our world—the world of magic. Total shit show.

Yet as I took in the gritted teeth, slightly wild eyes, and dark circles under the War horsewoman's eyes, I realized I hadn't considered that even if they'd saved our town before, that didn't mean they found it all easy. In fact, all of the Four looked more tired than powerful. And from the looks and sounds of it, this crowd was just getting started.

Maybe it was everything that had happened today that made me somehow give War a nod and assess the situation like I'd do any time we had to start triaging patients or dealing with a particularly crazy clinic day.

"Okay. You deal with the gods and whatever that is. Preferably somewhere else. We don't want one problem to bleed into the other," I told the Four. Nope, I wasn't even going to consider the fact that I was giving them orders. Gentle suggestions, maybe. Then I turned to the crowd and murmured to myself. "I'll deal with this."

I put my fingers between my lips and blew a sharp, loud whistle.

The crowd still looked toward the Four, pushing and shoving against each other as they tried to be heard. I caught what they were shouting more as parts of phrases rather than complete thoughts. "…Stole my land…They came after us…a vampire named Ted…fire and blood and flames and…"

The Four and their husbands moved away to join Loki and the leadership issues debate.

Despite a mild curiosity about what a vampire named Ted would ever do to anyone, I tried whistling again.

The sound was swallowed by the growing crowd.

Their mutterings grew louder and more unintelligible. "Why can't you… We need to… Where should we… You have to…" They pressed in closer, closer.

I stumbled back a few steps. Oh, hell. Maybe I was in over my head. If the Four couldn't—

A sudden flash and sparkle above shocked the crowd into silence as what appeared to have been a rock tossed into the air exploded into a shower of bubble and glitter.

Slim, warm fingers slid into mine.

I looked down to find Devi at my side.

"I lied," she said.

I frowned. "About why you were here?"

"That it was okay if you left. It wasn't. It isn't. So… I followed you. And I… I lied about Mr. Whiskers."

The crowd was starting to stir again, and I leaned in closer to hear Devi.

"What about my cat?"

"It isn't him I want to visit. Or see again. Or…get to know so that we can enjoy intimacies and sex. I would very much like to enjoy sex with you."

I rubbed my forehead a second, wondering if maybe I was lying unconscious somewhere and this was all a dream.

Devi leaned up, cupping my face. "I really like you, Frizzly. Seeing as my own family seems to want me dead, I suspect I'll be staying here for a time." She glanced at the crowd and frowned. "So, it would be best if we didn't let anyone destroy this place, wouldn't it?"

"It would indeed," I said, my voice rumbling. I squeezed her hand in mine, then turned to the crowd, raising my voice like I would to get any would-be med clinic riot under control. "All right. Here's what's going to happen. First, you're going to quiet down so you can all hear me. Come on now, back there. You'll want to listen to this."

"Don't make me turn you into bubbles!" Devi shouted beside me.

That, if not my words, quieted everyone down enough to look at her.

"We don't have to threaten them. We want to help them. And no turning them into bubbles or anything else, okay?" I said quietly.

She nodded, as though considering. "Oh. Okay." She beamed up at me.

I must have grown four feet right then.

Or maybe I found a cape that finally fit.

"All right, everyone. First, welcome to Beckwell. I'm Frizzly, and I'm going to make sure we sort everything and everyone out today, okay? It's going to take some time, and it will require some patience. But we will get to all of you today, you have my word." I spotted five familiar figures in my periphery.

Mr. Jenklow bent over his cane, Mr. Einar clapping him on the back, evidently congratulating themselves on their latest scheme. Mr. Liko still looked like he'd eaten something sour, Mr. Chaimek was winking at the ladies, and Mr. Zaki seemed to be trying to cower behind the bunch of them.

They didn't think they were getting out of this that easy, did they?

My lips curved into what some might have called a vengeful smile. "Okay, first off, let's get you organized according to your needs. Mr. Einar," I called.

Mr. Einar's smile slipped a little.

Mine only grew. "Everyone back there, see that tall gentleman with the great head of white hair? Mr. Einar, why don't you give everyone a wave."

Mr. Einar shook his head rapidly before the crowd shifted and turned to him. He pasted on that former-mayor smile and waved to the crowd.

"Excellent. Now, if you have issues with property claims or concerns about property ownership, such as if a castle has appeared in the middle of your field—or a field appeared around your castle—I'd like you to go form a line near Mr. Einar."

There was movement as people excused themselves and shifted through the crowd, emptying it of any of the faces familiar to me. But with a line forming next to Mr. Einar, the crowd turned back to me expectantly.

"Great work everyone. Thank you all for being so cooperative. Okay, next we're going to meet Mr. Jenklow, back there with the cane, and all of you who are seeking refuge here in Beckwell. Mr. Jenklow, give the crowd a wave so they know where to form the next line…"

It took all five of the Shades and nearly thirty minutes, but together, with Devi, we got everyone organized and moving out of the four-way stop. Vehicles dispersed in the directions Chief Quilan told them to park. People followed their Shade.

Doc Quilan gave me a thumbs-up from where he was standing with the others working on their own problem, and his wife blew me two-handed kisses that I suspected was influenced by their two baby twins.

Vehicle traffic moved off in groups toward the Cow Palace for refugees still seeking lodging.

Mr. Chaimek, followed by cell phones and even a few video cameras, led his group off on a tour.

Mr. Einar and Chief Quilan led the group with property claims back toward the community hall, squeezed between the library and the Senior Center off behind us.

Devi walked beside me, her hand still in mine as we headed toward the Cow Palace, leading our own group of people, most of them refugees to Beckwell looking for shelter, help, and hope. Getting everyone separated and temporarily averting the crisis was only the start of the solution. But it was something I could help with. I glanced at Mr. Jenklow, who gave me a wink.

"Hey, Devi," I said, still feeling ten feet tall. "I, uh, don't suppose maybe, if you're sticking around, that you might be up for a date?"

She blinked up at me, and I could see her cycling through her definitions before she frowned. "You mean, assign a specific time and place to something?"

"Uh, no. I mean, maybe go for a ride on Edith, dinner, maybe watch a movie together. They do movies every Saturday at the Senior Center in the dining hall," I added quickly, in case she thought I meant invite her back privately to my place. Which, of course, was what I actually wanted. She had mentioned sex, after all.

She beamed back at me, then quickly leaned up and pressed her lips to my jaw, before dropping away, her face turning bright pink. "I, uh, I mean—"

But her gaze was tugged away, and her smile quickly faded.

I followed the direction of her gaze as a tall, slim figure broke away from our group, cutting around the community hall and making a direct line toward the Senior Center.

"What is it?"

Her frown deepened. "I swear I…" The color blanched from her face as she swung on me. "It looked like one of my coworkers. Someone who used to work at USELESS and took the buyout when I did. You remember what Mr. Jenklow said, about if my mission failed—"

"They'd just try again," I murmured, my gaze darting up, searching for the slim figure. I dropped her hand and stalked after the stranger. Then broke into a run.

"Where are you going? What about these people, son?" Mr. Jenklow called after me.

"The Center. Another attack," I shouted back. "Get help!" Then I ran as fast as I could.

"Frizzly, wait!" Devi cried.

I could hear her racing after me, but I couldn't slow down.

I'd never been a great athlete. It takes a lot of energy and muscle to get stone—and the weight of stone—moving. But the thing is, once I was moving, there was also a hell of a lot that could be said for momentum. Which was why somehow, I managed to overtake the skinny guy, slamming into him and taking him to the floor just as we entered the glass doors into the Center's atrium.

We grappled with each other, the little wiry guy stronger than he looked. Our grunts and curses combined with us twisting and turning. Each of us fought for dominance, to get on top. Every twist gave me glimpses of our wide-eyed and growing audience of silver-haired residents.

"Get out of here!" I shouted at Devi as I saw her, puffing, come through the door.

My skinny opponent held a glowing orb that looked like the one Devi had been given.

Time seemed to slow.

Devi's eyes widened as she turned back toward the door and ran outside. Thank the gods. At least she'd be safe…and not make things inadvertently worse.

My opponent tossed the glowing orb in the air. It glowed and flickered all kinds of different colors in a very bad kind of way, in a way that it hadn't for Devi.

Maybe it'd just been a day. Maybe it was the brief look I got at the growing fear on the faces of the residents who seemed to be putting together what that orb was…but would never be able to get away fast enough. Residents in my town. My people. My responsibility.

Whatever it was, I scrambled to my feet and barely thought through my next actions other than a brief prayer to whatever troll gods there were that trolls really were immune to most magic. I dove and covered the orb with my body just as it landed on the floor.

All I saw was the brilliant flash of multi-colored light, a lick of heat. I pictured Devi's face, her overjoyed smile after our ride. And then…nothing.

Chapter Nine

THE FIRST THING I saw as my eyes flickered and blurs cleared to shapes and forms, finally clearing to reveal people, was Devi's beautiful face staring down at me. The warmth of her hands soaked through my skin where they framed my face. Tear tracks stained her face, her eyes over-bright, and she choked on a sob.

Huh. So, had the troll magic-immunity worked then?

"Am I dead?" I said, my voice croaky. Sun streamed in through the Senior Center atrium skylights, and the tile felt cool against my back. My legs were inordinately heavy, and I had to think about them to feel anything at all. Same went for my arms and hands. That couldn't be good.

"Not anymore," Devi said with a small, tremulous smile.

Um…

Another face—the small, pointed face of the Death horsewoman—leaned over me, and she waved a hand. "Give it a minute. Your body has to get used to the whole being alive part again. You're lucky we were nearby…and that I can't handle any more dead people right now.

Everyone gets a free pass until we figure out what we're supposed to do with all of them."

Assessing the situation and what I could feel of my body, I lay flat on my back on the tiled Senior Center atrium floor. Admittedly, I'd been laid out like this before, but that was usually at a bar. Aches and pains began to prick and throb all over my body, proving jumping on that explosive had consequences.

"Are we safe?" I asked. I struggled to sit up, but my body didn't want to cooperate. The best I could do was turn my head slightly. "What about the residents? The refugees?"

"You're the one who took the brunt of the blast. Because of that, everyone else walked away with minor cuts and bruises," Mal, the police chief, said, leaning in behind his wife, the Death horsewoman. "Everyone has been pretty worried about you, and the rest will wait. Just give it a minute. Take it from me, big guy. The whole coming back to life thing is confusing. And it hurts. But it beats the alternative." He turned. "Daniel, can we get him upright at least? It can't be comfortable down there."

The police chief took my hands and pulled while Doc Daniel helped lever me up from behind, studying my eyes as I sat upright, and my vision swam again. Those aches and pains grew, too.

"How you doing, Frizz?" the doc asked, not taking his hand from my back.

"Not dead. Apparently," I croaked. It was an effort, but I managed to move my arm enough to shrug off his hand. "I'm good."

He snorted. "Full check-up in the morning, you hear me?"

I was saved from having to answer as he, his brother, and the Death horsewoman stood and stepped aside.

Seemed like there was a line-up.

Mr. Jenklow, with popping knees and a small grimace, used his cane to get down to my level, his bright blue eyes twinkling. "Good work for proving me right, son. Liko is never going to live this down. I knew you were the one to help get people organized and get Beckwell moving in the right direction."

"Glad I could help. But next time if you need help, just ask. Leave my cat and Devi out of it," I said, my throat raw and scratchy.

The old man chuckled but agreed to nothing as one of the other horsewomen helped him up.

Feeling started to return to my limbs, and it wasn't the warm, fuzzy kind. It was possible my body hurt more than after being dissolved and resolidified by Devi's grandmother.

"What were you thinking? If the Four hadn't come running at the explosion, you might have been dead forever," Devi said, another tear following the track of what looked like others. She brushed at her face impatiently, turning a distressed scowl on me.

I shrugged. "Sometimes, I guess you can't just play it safe. Sometimes, you have to take the risks and do what you can to help those you care about. I couldn't let any of the residents, my town, or you get hurt because of that blast." Sometimes, maybe you just ran out there and tried to make a difference, whether the cape and tights fit or not.

"So, you decided that throwing yourself on top of an explosive was a good idea?"

I tried to shrug, but that hurt too much. "There wasn't a lot of time to think it through. I hoped maybe my troll magic immunity might soften the blast." I looked around. "What about the skinny guy who brought the bomb here, your former coworker? Did he get away?"

A flush climbed Devi's cheekbones. "Oh. About that. So…remember what happened to the eagle?"

"Uh, yeah?"

She nodded toward a straight-backed wooden chair near one of the char-stained sofas.

"It turns out I really am rubbish at the whole destruction thing. But transmogrification? That I'm *very* good at, even in a panic. When you grabbed the bomb and told me to run, I barely even thought of it, and poof! Chair." She considered the wood chair with a small frown. "Although… I was trying for a statue. I should turn him back into a man…when I figure out how. I was thinking of asking Bibiji for some help."

The Death horsewoman cleared her throat, shooting Mr. Jenklow a dirty look before looking at Devi. "About help… I hear you're good at creating reality bubble things, or whatever they're called. Before the Veils went down, a lot of the dead existed in places like hell, purgatory, and the like, which were bubbles within other worlds and the Gray. When the Veils fell, those places went with it, booting the dead out and leaving a big mess. What I'm saying is, if you could help create some new realities, a lot of people including me would be very grateful."

Devi just blinked a moment or two, glancing back at me a second as she bit her lip. "I, well… I am going to need a new job. But…you're sure you'd trust me with something as important as this?"

Death rolled her eyes, but a small smile pulled at her lips. "I'm pretty sure you're about the only one able *and* willing to do it, period. We'd be damned lucky to have you."

Devi's smile lit up her face, and she turned that brilliance on me. "Did you hear that, Frizzly? I have a new job! And this time I know I'm going to…" She let her voice trail off with a small frown, seemingly considering something a moment before she straightened her shoulders and lifted her chin. "You know what? Whether my family or anyone else believes it, *I* know I'm the right person for this job." She gave me a small, slightly shy grin. "Plus, it means I have even more reason to stay in Beckwell."

That tiny flutter of hope whispered through me again.

"I'm sure Frizzly could also use the help organizing all the new arrivals in Beckwell," Mr. Jenklow added.

"Anyone helping to handle some of the paperwork on the new arrivals is a saint in my book," the police chief added.

Admin work. Helping manage people with kindness and honesty. People who would see that anyone—including a half-troll and former biker—could help. Besides, I was a hell of a lot better at the organizing part then some of the other heroes in town, including the Four and my boss. A slow smile pulled across my face. "Yeah. I'd be more than happy to handle that," I said. "If you wouldn't mind helping a guy up?"

The police chief grinned at me and offered me a hand. The doc offered me his, and together they hauled me to my feet. The world whirled only a little this time, but Devi was right there, tucking herself against my side and helping lead me to the slightly charred sofa. I sank gratefully down into it, just Devi and me while Death, the doc, the police chief, and Mr. Jenklow chatted before starting to move off.

I glanced down to where Devi had twined her small fingers in mine, and I smoothed my thumb over her fingers. Those fireworks were still there, and something deeper, something more than just physical attraction. It'd been a hell of a day, and we'd managed to survive... Well, mostly, considering I wasn't dead anymore. Finally, Devi and I had a quiet moment alone.

"Uh, Frizzly?" she said quietly, causing me to look up and meet her dark gaze, catch the pretty flush on her face.

I tried not to squeeze her fingers too tight in mine. "Yeah?"

"Could we go on our date now?"

I blinked. "Now? Like… right now?"

She nodded. "Yes. Right now, if you're up to it." She frowned a little, as though considering her words before she continued. "If I've learned anything, it's that things can change quickly here in Beckwell. In case they change again, in case the Guardians attack tonight, or we have to go try and save anyone else, I thought, well, I'd like to go on that date you mentioned. The time spent together. Romantic time." She flushed like crazy, ducking her head.

I reached gently and lifted her chin, waiting until her gaze met mine. I'd never been forward, never been very good with women or saying the right thing. Then again, I'd never been one for trying to play the hero either. Not until I'd met Devi.

"Mr. Whiskers really likes you. I really like you. If you're willing to try, I would very much like to go out on that date with you. And if you're going to be around for a while, I'd like to, uh, give a relationship a try." Because how else did you say you were pretty sure she was "the one" without freaking her out?

The way her face lit up said I'd said the right thing, and I knew it for sure when she leaned forward and pressed her soft lips to mine. She tasted of sunshine and spice, of rainbows and hope, with just a dash of chaos.

She pulled back enough to grin at me again, cupping my jaw with her hand. "This means that now we'll know each other better and more intimate activities will be expected, right?"

I could barely swallow, let alone speak, so I just nodded, my heart and my head too full of images of us together.

"Excellent," she said, and leaned forward to continue to kiss me.

Somewhere, in the back of my mind not occupied with kissing Devi, flashed the idea that I was lucky to have a cat who wanted to kill me. Thanks to Mr. Whiskers and almost dying today, and thanks to Devi, I think I'd finally figured out how to live.

A Note...

DEAR READER,

I hope you've enjoyed Frizzly and Devi, and meeting the Shades of Beckwell. I'm so excited to finally share this expanded Beckwell with you and hope you love it – and this loveable group of men who prove heroes come in all shapes, sizes, and ages.

Want more of the Shades? Find them next in the full-length novel *Shade for Love*, available October 2021 and featuring that elusive original leader of the Shades: an immortal warrior and the Baba Yaga descendent he falls for.

As a special bonus, sign up for my newsletter at www.shellychalmers.com and get a FREE exclusive Shades novelette, *Alchemy*. You can also contact me there – I love hearing from readers!

Otherwise, until next time, I hope you join me and the Shades as we head off on a wild new adventure to defeat the Guardians. We'll make some mischief, meet the couples finding love, and have some fun. Oh, and probably try to end the world a few times. It's Beckwell. What did you expect? Peace and quiet? 😉

All the best, and wishing you the magic of the everyday,

SHELLY

Also by Shelly Chalmers

The Shades of Beckwell Series:

Trolled

Alchemy

Shade for Love (Available October 2021)

The Sisters of the Apocalypse Series:

Must Love Plague

Must Love Famine

Must Love Death

Must Love War

www.ingramcontent.com/pod-product-compliance
Ingram Content Group UK Ltd.
Pitfield, Milton Keynes, MK11 3LW, UK
UKHW040010200726
13854UKWH00001B/122

9 781777 888107